Secrets
The
Swamp Keeps

Secrets
The
Swamp
Keeps

A NOVEL

Jon-Patric Nelson

For information, contact:
NelsonDPT, LLC Publishing
Nashville, TN
jonpatricnelson@gmail.com

Cover design by Jon-Patric Nelson
ISBN: 979-8-9860596-5-5

Printed in the United States of America
First Edition: 2025

10 9 8 7 6 5 4 3 2 1

This one is for Noel Morris.
I know you're rooting for me.

"Would you rather be at peace with the world
and at war with yourself? Or at war with the world
and at peace with yourself?"
—Nipsey Hussle

"Having a superpower has nothing to do with
the ability to fly or jump, or superhuman strength.
The truest superpowers are the ones we all possess:
willpower, integrity, and most importantly, courage."
—Jason Reynolds

Secrets
The
Swamp Keeps

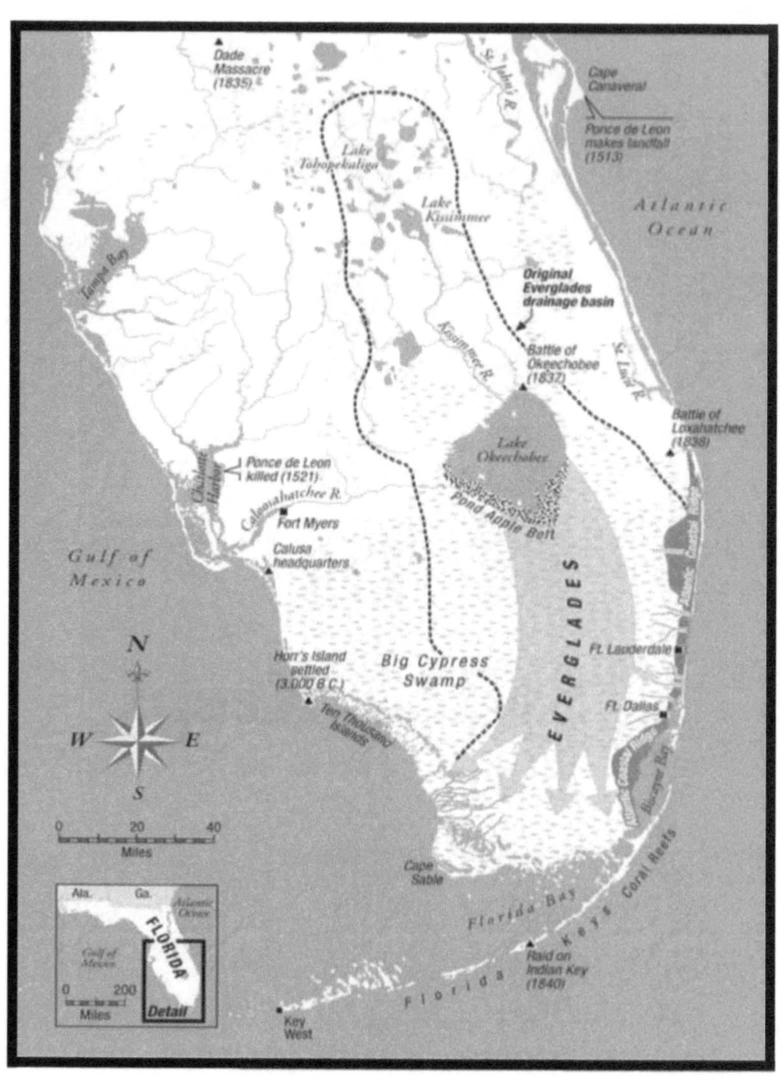

Map of South Florida

Big Cypress Swamp (2019)

I'm a little terrified.
I really don't wanna see another dead body.
Shot. Stabbed. Strangled.
But these 2 legged animals won't stop.

A man came with a girl the other night.
She tried to run but his grip was too tight.
Her body floated for three days.
Three fuckin' days.
Before flashlights and caution tapes showed up.
That's the only time they show up.
2 legged animals w/ badges on their chests reflected by
the moonlight.
I can almost count on it.
Sometimes the next day.
Other times...
Yeah...other times they dig up skeletons.
So long...
So long I on't e'en remember if the skin was fair or full of
melanin.
I hate it. Holding a body that don't belong here.
That belongs with them.
Trauma, I got PTSD.

I've been here for years.
Things used to be different.

I remember Carlos.
He lived here with his family.
The Calusas, they were natives—Native Americans.
I accepted them, they accepted me. All of me.
They didn't treat me like a morgue.
They had no secrets to hide.

Shhh, keep quiet...here comes another one.
See...They trust me but then they run.
I'm exhausted.
Holding their secrets ain't really all that fun.

Prologue

Oak-Haven, Florida (2019)

The swamp had been here longer than anyone could remember.

Before the highways, before the tourists, before the strip malls spread across South Florida like a rash. It had been here when the Calusa people fished these waters, when they built their shell mounds and lived in harmony with the gators and cypresses. Back then, the swamp was sacred. A place of life. Now it was a graveyard with a pulse. The swamp remembered Carlos and his family—they accepted these waters, understood them, respected them. They didn't treat it like a morgue. They had no secrets to hide. But that was centuries ago. Now the swamp held different memories. Bodies weighted down with cinder blocks. Blood mixing with the brackish water. The two-legged animals always came at night. The darkness hid them, the murky water kept their secrets.

Palm trees swayed, and the sun shone relentlessly, a shadow waited. It played tag and hide-and-seek — children's games, twisted into something far from innocent. A whisper in the wind—a ripple in the still waters surrounding the Everglades. A chilling presence that left a mark on all it touched—*tag, you're it!*

It wasn't just the heat, the oppressive humidity that clung to the skin like a shroud, or the mosquitoes that whined their incessant, bloodthirsty song. The Everglades held its breath, a vast, green lung exhaling secrets on the wind. And those who lived on its fringes, those who thought they knew its rhythms, its dangers, were often the most surprised by what it could conceal, what it could unleash. The games played here were not for the faint of heart, and the stakes were higher than anyone in their right mind would ever gamble.

Chapter 1-Autumn

Someone had broken into Autumn's car, leaving a stuffed animal with a razor blade stitched into its belly. Sage found it first—nearly slicing her hand open.

They'd both stared at the blood on the blade, understanding the message: *We can reach you anywhere. We can hurt the people you love.*

Autumn walked to the kitchen window, pulled the curtain back an inch. The black sedan was still there. Same missing hubcap. Same tinted windows that revealed nothing.

Her phone buzzed. Unknown number.

You have 48 hours to forget what you saw.

She deleted it, just like the other seventeen messages. Her thumb hovered over 911, just like every other time. But what would she say?

They'd ask why she hadn't come forward sooner. They'd ask if she had proof. They'd ask if she was sure she wasn't just paranoid, stressed, a single mom seeing conspiracies where there were only coincidences.

And while they asked, while they investigated, while they decided whether to believe her—Gabriel would be vulnerable. Sage would be vulnerable. Anyone she'd spoken to would be a target.

The sedan's headlights flicked on.

Autumn's breath caught. She stepped back from the window, her heart hammering against her ribs like something trying to escape.

"Mommy?" Gabriel appeared beside her, dragging his stuffed elephant. "Can we have mac and cheese?"

She looked down at his upturned face, so innocent, so trusting. What kind of world had she brought him into? What kind of mother put him in danger because she couldn't keep her mouth shut, couldn't mind her business, couldn't just let powerful men do powerful things?

"Yeah, baby." She lifted him onto her hip, breathing in his little-boy smell of playground dirt and strawberry shampoo. "We can have whatever you want."

The sedan pulled away from the curb.

Autumn watched it disappear around the corner, counted to sixty, then checked the window again. Empty street. No headlights. No watchers. But she knew they'd be back.

That night, Sage and Autumn bolted their bedroom doors and left the hallway light burning. Autumn whispered, "They know where we live." And Sage couldn't tell if her fingers trembled from anger or pure fear.

The next day Autumn found a Polaroid on her windshield—her walking home, unaware, somebody trailing behind her in the frame. She looked around before stuffing it in her purse.

"What's that mommy? "

"Nothing, baby. Let's take you to grandma."

"But I don't wanna go to grandma's," whined Gabriel.

"Just for a few hours, Gabriel. Mommy gotta take care of some things."

She scooped him up and gave him one of her big mommy hugs. His tiny arms clasped around her neck. She held on a little longer, a little tighter than usual. Water filled her eyes.

"We'll go to Dinosaur World. Pinky promise."

Her pinky wrapped around his.

"Okay, let's go baby."

Gabriel hopped into the backseat.

Autumn dropped him off to her mother before making her way back to her apartment.

She was at a red light when she felt something smash into the back of her car. The impact jerked her forward, slamming her forehead into the steering wheel. Dazed, she looked into the rear view mirror.

It was a pick up truck. She reached for her cell phone to call 911. Her thumb punched 9 but before she could hit the number 1 the door swung open and a large figure latched onto her.

***

"Ahhh! No! Please, stop!"

Autumn's bare feet tore against twisted roots as she sprinted, desperate and wild. Branches snatched at her skin, the swamp's damp air filling her lungs with dread. Behind, his footsteps thundered—steady, relentless, a darkness with a human face overtaking her heartbeat. Breath ragged, she darted between the cypress knees, not daring to look back. Behind her, the man followed. His steps louder than her gasping breath. Each stride crushing damp leaves underfoot. He was a force of nature in worn boots and dark, sweat-stained clothes, his breathing steady and calm. The air around him hummed with a dark energy, a predatory focus that narrowed the world down to the single goal of capturing his prey. There was no hesitation in his movements, no flicker of doubt, only a terrifying efficiency. He tore her t-shirt from her body. Her breasts were exposed. She screamed. Her skin shivered as she stumbled. Her face slammed into the mud. Her arms tied tightly behind her back.

Before she could rise, his silhouette mounted over her. His hand yanked her hair, dragging her to her knees. Tears mixed with the mud on her face, a silent plea. "Please," she managed. "I have a son. Please." But this man didn't believe in mercy.

A branding iron, glowing red-hot, hissed in his gloved hand.

"Tag," he said, voice flat as the dead water around them. "You're it."

The iron inched closer, its heat licking at her skin. She thrashed wildly, her body writhing in every direction, but his grip was unyielding. Tears streamed down her face as she braced for the searing pain. The scent of charred flesh filled the air, mingling with her screams as the iron pressed against her forearm, leaving a permanent mark.

Her body collapsed. Unconscious. But alive. Barely. Her chest rose and fell in shallow, uneven breaths, her body clinging to life.

The man turned to the Big Cypress Swamp.

Ima dump this bitch right here, he thought.

Somewhere deeper in the swamp, a lone alligator slid into the water, ripples disturbing the mirror-like surface. Mosquitoes buzzed in a cloud, a constant, irritating presence. He slung Autumn's 115-pound frame over his shoulder and trudged forward. His boots sank into the soft muck. Reaching the edge of the water, he flung her body into the dark. The water was black as oil, still as glass. The swamp rippled. For a moment, nothing.

Then, a gator surfaced. Its yellow, unblinking eyes gleamed with hunger as it glided toward her. The alligator's massive jaws opened, revealing rows of jagged teeth. The water erupted in a violent splash as the reptile clamped down on her torso. Autumn dissolved beneath the water's skin, the ripples spreading outward, swallowing all traces of her. The swamp went still again. It always did.

Chapter 2- Sage

Sage sat on the edge of the couch, her hands wringing a tissue until it was a little more than shredded fibers. She hadn't looked up since the detectives arrived, her eyes fixed on the coffee table.

"Autumn told me she was scared," her voice cracked. Her hands clutched a Styrofoam cup, but she didn't sip. Petite, doe-eyed, jittery—she hadn't slept in days.

"Scared of what?" Detective Mason leaned forward, his brows furrowed. The fluorescent light overhead buzzed faintly.

"She said someone was following her. At first, I thought she was being paranoid...she was always anxious. But then... she came home one night with a black eye.

Her shirt was ripped, and there was blood. I told her to call the police, but she begged me not to."

Detective Monroe, arms crossed, watched silently.

"She said..." Sage swallowed hard. "She said she couldn't afford to."

Mason's jaw tightened. "Why not?"

"She had secrets. Things she said would ruin her if they came out." The girl's eyes dropped to her lap. "She thought staying quiet would keep her safe."

Mason exchanged a glance with his partner, Detective Monroe.

"Do you think she was right?" asked Monroe.

The girl shook her head, tears spilling down her cheeks. "If she hadn't known anything, maybe she'd still be alive."

Chapter 3- Mason

The sun slanted through the dusty blinds of the Oak-Haven Sheriff's Department, illuminating motes dancing in the stagnant air. Detective Mason leaned back in his oversized leather chair, the springs groaning—195 pounds of muscle earned in the gym, not behind a desk. Across from him sat Officer Ramirez, a younger man with a perpetually tired look and a notepad open on his lap, though he hadn't written anything in the last ten minutes. They were reviewing the initial reports on Autumn's disappearance, a case that had quickly escalated to a homicide, and one that was already growing cold.

"Anything new, Ray?" Mason asked. He rubbed a hand over his face, the stubble rough against his palm. The paperwork on his desk seemed to multiply overnight, each file a reminder of a life interrupted, a mystery unsolved.

Ramirez sighed, rubbing his hair.

"Nothing, Detective. We re-interviewed the roommate, Sage. Twice."

He flipped through his notes.

"Same story—Autumn was scared, black eye, no details. But she doesn't know who was following her, or why."

"And the boyfriend?" asked Mason.

"Trevor? Still grieving, obviously. Says he hadn't seen Autumn much lately; they had drifted apart. Confirmed the black eye story, said Autumn told him she'd just fallen. He didn't push it, didn't want to cause a fight." Ramirez paused. "Seems genuine, the grief. But you never know."

Mason grunted. "Grief could be a powerful mask. What about the scene? Anything else from the swamp?"

"Negative. Search teams went over that area near the west entrance again. Nothing but mud, cypress knees, and gators. Whatever happened, the swamp swallowed it whole."

They were deep in thought, broken only by the distant ring of a phone. Mason's attention drifted to the corkboard on the wall, covered with photos and notes related to their active cases. Autumn's face, young and smiling in her college ID photo. Twenty-three years old. Nursing student. Single mother. Her smile in that photo held no hint she'd end up in a swamp. It was pinned next to a blurry surveillance image from a convenience store robbery. The contrast was evident, a reminder of the different kinds of darkness they dealt with.

"You know," Ramirez said, breaking the silence, "I was looking through the old incident reports from that area. The Big Cypress Swamp. Ramirez riffled through memory and notepad.

"The swamp keeps its mouth shut, mostly," he muttered. "Last time anyone vanished, it was old poachers fighting over airboats. This time, though—feels like the mud itself is hiding something."

"Get to the point, Ray."

"There was a report, about six months ago," Ramirez continued, flipping through his notepad, though the information seemed to be in his head.

"A disturbance. Near the west entrance. Some kind of confrontation. The responding officer didn't find much, just some tire tracks, a few footprints that weren't from boots. Said it looked like someone had been dragged."

Mason's eyes narrowed. "Dragged? Why wasn't this flagged?"

"Low priority at the time, Detective. No victims, no witnesses. Just a 'disturbance.' The officer figured it was just some poachers fighting over territory."

"Who was the responding officer?"

"Officer Miller. He's on vacation this week."

"Figures." Mason leaned forward.

"Were there any names? Any vehicles identified?"

"No names. The tire tracks were from a truck, nothing specific. The footprints... Miller noted they were unusual. Not work boots, not sneakers. Said they looked almost... bare, but with some kind of impression around the toes, like claws."

"Claws?" Mason scoffed. "That darn Miller been reading too many comic books?"

"I know, it sounds crazy," Ramirez said, shrugging. "But that's what he wrote. *Footprints consistent with bare feet, with claw-like impressions around the toes.*"

Mason was silent, his mind sifting through the details. *A disturbance six months ago, near the west entrance of the Big Cypress. Tire tracks from a truck. Footprints, one set of which looked like someone had been dragged, and another with a bizarre description. No victim, no witnesses, so it was dismissed.* But now, six months later, Autumn was found dead in the same general area, a victim of a violent act, her body bearing a strange mark.

"Get Miller's full report," Mason ordered, sitting up straight. "And see if there were any other incidents reported in that area around the same time. Anything at all, no matter how small. I gotta reach out to Autumn's family."

"Will do, Detective." Ramirez finally started writing in his notepad, the pen scratching against the paper.

Mason stood up and walked to the window, looking out at the passing cars. The world outside the dusty office was growing darker.

***

Mason drove down the back roads of Oak-Haven, windows down, the swamp's musk heavy in the air. The streets on this part of Oak-Haven were different from the manicured lawns and gated communities Detective Mason had seen on the edges of town. This part didn't make the tourist brochures. Here, the houses were smaller, closer together. Kids darted barefoot through cracked streets, dodging cars and stray dogs. A rusted pickup rumbled past, its headlights slicing through the morning fog. The smell of fried fish and something else floated into their nostrils.

Mason and Monroe parked their unmarked sedan and stepped out.

Monroe loosened his tie. "Hot as hell out here."

"It's Florida. It's always hot." Mason surveyed the street. Several houses had bars on the windows. One had a busted porch light. Another had what looked like bullet holes in the siding, patched over with mismatched paint.

They were here to follow up on a few leads, to knock on doors and ask questions about Autumn. To see if anyone had seen or heard anything out of the ordinary in the days leading up to her disappearance.

But the response they got was not what they expected. Doors remained closed, curtains twitched as faces peered out, then disappeared. When someone opened a door, the exchange was brief, the answers guarded.

"We're just asking a few questions about a missing girl, Autumn Hayes," Mason said to a tired woman balancing a baby on her hip.

The woman shifted her weight, gaze flitting down the street as if trouble might be watching.

"Ain't seen nothin'," she said, voice flat. The door closed before Mason could thank her.

At another house, a young man eyed them with suspicion. "Twelve," he muttered under his breath. "What do you want?"

"Just trying to find some information," Monroe said, his voice neutral. "We're investigating a homicide."

The young man's expression hardened. "Homicide? Suddenly y'all care? What about all the other stuff that happens around here? The stuff y'all don't bother with?" He shook his head. "Nah, I ain't got nothin' to say." He, too, closed the door.

Mason exchanged a glance with Monroe. "They're not making it easy," Monroe commented.

"They have their reasons," Mason replied, his voice thoughtful. He knew these streets. He knew the history of police presence in these neighborhoods, the broken promises, the heavy-handed tactics, the times when problems weren't addressed unless they spilled over into more affluent areas. He knew the sense of being watched, of being targeted, even when you hadn't done anything wrong.

"Look, Detective," Monroe said, a hint of frustration in his tone. "We can't force people to talk. If they don't want to help, then-"

"Then we keep trying," Mason interrupted. "We have to. This girl, Autumn, deserves justice. And if we don't earn their trust, if we don't show them we're serious, we're not going to get anywhere."

Mason pulled up to a shotgun house at the end of a rutted lane. Detective Monroe waited by the porch, tapping ash off a cigarette as Mason knocked on the door.

"Anything?" Monroe asked, climbing the steps.

"Lady said she heard a girl scream two nights ago. Thought it was teenagers messing around. Didn't call it in," responded Mason.

"Shit. Ain't nobody roun' here talkin'. Folks keep their secrets locked up tighter than a gator's jaw," Monroe muttered.

Mason gave Monroe a side eye. "C'mon man, too early."

He knocked on the next door. An old man peeked out.

"Sheriff's Department," Mason said, showing his badge. "Mind if we ask you a few questions?"

The man stepped aside. "Yeah, come in 'fore them skeeters tear y'all asses up," warned the man.

The swamp buzzed behind them, a chorus of hidden things.

Inside, the air was stale with fried fish and old wood. The man spoke. "Didn't see much. Heard the splash. Then nothin'."

They continued down the street, knocking on doors, offering polite greetings and patient explanations. Cautiously, hesitantly, a few people began to talk.

An elderly woman sat on her porch, fanning herself with a church program. Mason approached slowly, showing his badge from a respectful distance.

"Ma'am, I'm Detective Mason. Mind if I ask you a few questions?"

She squinted at him, then at Monroe standing by. "You the police."

"Yes, ma'am."

"Whatchu want?"

"We're investigating a death. Young woman named Autumn Hayes. Lived over on Palmetto. We're trying to find out if anyone saw or heard anything unusual earlier this morning."

The woman's fan stopped moving. "That girl they found in the swamp?"

"Yes, ma'am."

"Hmph." She resumed fanning. "I heard a scream. Thought it was teenagers messing around, so I didn't call it in." Her eyes met his, and Mason saw the guilt there. "Should've called."

Mason kept his voice gentle. "You didn't know, ma'am. But anything you can tell me now might help."

"It was a girl's scream. Scared. Real scared." She pointed down the street. "Came from that direction. Toward the swamp"

Mason made a note. "What time?"

"Past midnight. I was up late watching my stories on the DVR."

"Did you see any vehicles? Anyone walking?"

She shook her head. "Just heard the scream. Then nothing."

Mason handed her his card. "If you remember anything else, call me directly. Anytime."

She took the card, studied it. "You think you gonna find who did it?"

"Yes, ma'am. I do."

"Hmph." She tucked the card into her housecoat. "Most times, you people don't solve nothin' in this neighborhood. But I hope you do. That girl had a baby, didn't she?"

"Yes, ma'am."

The woman's expression hardened. "Then you better find whoever did this. That baby needs to know his mama's death meant something."

At the end of the street they encountered a weathered bridge that led to a trail next to the swamp. The water under the bridge moved slow as syrup, thick with vegetation. Monroe pulled out another cigarette. He took a draw and flicked ashes from his Lucky Strike into the swirling current below the rickety bridge.

"So, a black truck, seen late at night," Monroe mused. "And someone heard an argument."

Mason nodded. "They're small pieces, Monroe, but they fit... a pattern. The people here, they see things. They hear things. But none of it points to a name, a face. The truth is out there, in those reluctant words, but for now we have nothin'. "

Each small piece of information felt like a victory, a crack in the wall of mistrust. Mason knew it would take time, but he was determined to chip away at that wall, to bridge the gap between law enforcement and this community. He knew it wasn't just about solving a crime; it was about showing people that their voices mattered, that their stories were worth hearing, that their lives were just as valuable as anyone else's in Oak-Haven.

As they made their way through the neighborhood back to their car, Mason paused, watching a group of children playing in the street. He thought about what it would take to truly make a difference, to change the relationship between the police and the people they were supposed to protect. He knew it wasn't just about arresting criminals; it was about building trust, about showing respect, about acknowledging the pain and the history that often stood between them. And he knew it would take more than just showing up after something bad had happened. It would take being present, being visible, being a part of the community, even when there wasn't a case to be solved.

Chapter 4- Bryson

Bryson was fixing breakfast when he heard a knock at his front door. Scrambled eggs still steaming in the pan, coffee brewing. The Ring camera popped up on his phone. It displayed two men. They stood shoulder to shoulder on the front steps of the porch, their hands grasped around their belts, showcasing their badges. Both men wore crisp white dress shirts . One with a blazer, the other a hunter green tie. The universal uniform of bad news. They were both tall. The Black man was statuesque, powerfully built. He was all bone structure and defined lines. The other, a bronze-colored White man. He was lean with a neatly trimmed gray goatee.

A familiar knot of anxiety churned in Bryson's gut. Seeing one of them—a Black man in his neatly pressed outfit—eased some of the tension. A small thing, but it registered. He still didn't like dealing with the police. Not any police. He'd had enough encounters, enough close calls, enough reminders that as a Black man, interactions with law enforcement were never simple, never truly safe. But seeing that Black face alongside the other man, offered a sliver of reassurance. Maybe, just maybe, this would be different. He flipped the deadbolt and opened the door a crack, the chain still engaged.

"Wassup, can I help y'all?" he asked, trying to project an air of calm he didn't feel.

The Black detective stepped forward.

"Sir, are you Bryson Hayes?" he asked, his sonorous voice carrying an edge of authority.

"Yes?" Bryson said.

"I'm Detective Mason and he's Detective Monroe. We'd like to sit down and speak with you."

"About what? This can't be about that speeding ticket I got last week?" Bryson asked. Mason did not respond. He looked over at his partner. Monroe lowered his head. The anxiety in Bryson's gut ramped up. Mason exhaled, and Bryson knew something had gone wrong.

"Is your sister's name Autumn Hayes?" he finally spoke.

The eggs were burning. Bryson could smell them, hear them hissing in the pan, but he couldn't move.

Couldn't breathe. The world had narrowed to Mason's mouth, to the words that were about to come out of it.

Bryson unhinged the chain from the door.

"Yeah, what's wrong with my sister?" Bryson asked. He trembled.

"Mr. Hayes, we need you to sit down."

"I'm fine standing. What about my sister?"

Mason took off his sunglasses. His eyes were kind, which was worse somehow. Worse than if they'd been cold.

"Mr. Hayes," Mason began, his voice carefully neutral, "We found a body in the Big Cypress Swamp earlier this morning. We believe it to be your sister, Autumn."

The words hit him in stages. Body. Swamp. Sister. They didn't fit together, couldn't fit together. Autumn was alive. She'd texted him three days ago about them never hanging out. She'd complained about her lab shift. She'd sent him a meme about bad drivers.

"Mr. Hayes." Monroe stepped forward. "We're very sorry for your loss."

Loss. The word clanged in his skull like a prison bell. Loss meant she was gone. Loss meant she wasn't coming back. Loss meant—

His knees gave out.

"No," Bryson managed to choke out, shaking his head in disbelief. "No, that's not... that's not possible."

He caught himself on the doorframe, but the world was tilting, rotating on an axis that didn't make sense anymore. The detectives were talking, saying things about identification, about next of kin, about the coroner's office, but their words were underwater sounds, muffled and distant.

A low, guttural sound escaped his throat, a sound that was half-sob, half-gasp.

"How?" he managed.

"We're still investigating—" responded Mason.

"How did she die?"

Chapter 5- Bryson

The rain came down steadily like it does on every funeral on TV. Dark clouds swallowed the sky, blanketing the world in a cold, gray caress. It was the sunshine state, so in the next five minutes, the sun would be reaching out to embrace everyone with a sweltering kiss. Summer days in Florida were always a tug-of-war between sun and storm, especially September during hurricane season.

A sea of black swallowed the cemetery, each figure a somber silhouette against the gray sky. Bryson stood stiffly among them, the rain soaking through the shoulders of his charcoal suit. His eyes remained locked on the glossy mahogany of the casket, its polished surface reflecting the dull light. To his side, Mrs. Hayes clenched the handle of her black umbrella, knuckles white, her head bowed so low that her chin nearly touched her chest.

The pastor's mournful baritone cut through the soft patter of rain. Autumn's casket sat on a green turf. Pastor George held a black book in his hands while reciting words from the pages. Every so often, he'd stop to wipe the raindrops from his glasses with a black cloth. His voice carried over and under the umbrellas, stimulating every eardrum in his presence. He closed the book and placed it underneath his arms. His endomorphic frame proceeded to the left side of the casket, his hand gently resting on the polished wood—and the sobs in the crowd intensified.

As Pastor George's words faded into the rain, Mrs. Hayes's gaze lingered on the casket, not with the blank sorrow everyone expected, but with a flash of something akin to anger. *Ay, Dios mío*, she thought, her lips moving silently. *Why her? Why take my bird while the vipers still crawl?* This wasn't just grief; it was outrage, a sense of injustice so profound it bordered on fury. In her culture, death wasn't simply an ending, but a transition, and to have her child torn away so violently, so unfairly, felt like a violation. She susurrated a prayer under her breath, a mixture of Spanish and Creole, a plea for guidance and retribution. The words weren't all gentle; some were sharp, almost accusatory, directed at a God who she felt had failed her.

She looked up as the pastor's voice amplified.

"Once Autumn Hayes returns to the dust from which she came, her soul shall return to heaven whence it came. Ashes to ashes, dust to dust. May her soul rest in eternal peace," he intoned, his voice balanced and resolute. When his final words faded, a petite funeral director in a sharp black blazer stepped forward. Her crimson lipstick stood vivid against her deep brown skin. She spoke calm and clear, dismissing the mourners with a polite nod toward closure no one wanted. As everyone dispersed, Bryson's focus lingered on the casket.

A small boy, his hand clasped in Mrs. Hayes', held a delicate rose in his right hand. Bryson turned to look at the boy.

"Unky, can I put it on Momma's box now?" His voice trembled, but the flower stayed firm in his grip. Bryson crouched, meeting his nephew's eyes.

"Of course, little man."

Though Gabriel was a bright four-year-old, he was too young to understand such a tragedy. When Mrs. Hayes had told him that his mommy went to sleep, he thought nothing of it. He wanted to give her a rose, mirroring the way she'd given him a teddy bear while he slept.

Gabriel shuffled forward. Bryson watched as his nephew stretched over the box. His two sizes too large blazer dragged against the top of the casket, soaking up the raindrops that settled. He placed the rose gently, the petals already drooping under the drizzle.

"That's my daughter in there. My baby girl," Mrs. Hayes sobbed, clutching Bryson's arm like it was all that kept her standing. He flinched at the raw edge of her voice. He'd heard it before, the same cracked grief when his father died — but grief never learned to hurt less.

"I'm so sorry for your loss. My thoughts are with you and your family," consoled an older man, his hand resting gently on Bryson's shoulder. The man's words did little to allay the agony in his soul. It wasn't that he didn't appreciate his gesture, he did. It's that his words were bromidic, exactly what you expect when someone dies. There was nothing the man could do to assuage his pain.

The light rain stopped stroking the leaves on the trees. Soon thereafter, a baby's wail drowned out all the conversations and soft sobs. Bryson collapsed his umbrella, twisted the strap around it, and fastened the clasp. With each step he took, the umbrella rubbed back and forth on his leg like a black cat yearning for attention.

With the funeral over and most people gone, only Bryson, Mrs. Hayes, Gabriel, the funeral crew, and Sage remained. A lot of Autumn's friends showed up for the service. Bryson couldn't say that for his family. Only a few showed and they didn't stick around for long either.

Little Gabriel stomped in a puddle. Water splashed up, speckling Mrs. Hayes's skirt. She flinched. "¡Basta, chico!" she snapped—the Spanish sharp with her Dominican lilt, grief frayed into frustration. Gabriel's face crumpled, and a loud cry escaped his lips. Tears streamed down his cheeks. He buried his face in Mrs. Hayes's skirt, sobbing uncontrollably.

"I'm sorry baby," said Mrs. Hayes.

Gabriel took a pregnant pause, then began to scream louder.

"Take him to the car mom. I'll be there soon," Bryson said. She nodded in agreement, her hand stroking Gabriel's damp curls.

"Okay, mi niño. We'll be in the car when you're ready."

Gabriel's cries faded as they walked away. Bryson stepped toward the casket. He laid his hand on the casket, the cold biting into his palm, seeping through as he felt it in his bones.His baby sister was gone. Memories came in waves—her laugh, her smile—but the illusion broke as quickly as it came.

Sage was on the other end of the casket. She walked right up to Bryson and stood next to him.

"Hey, I'm Sage, Autumn's homegirl. She told me all about you," Sage said with a small smile.

"Hey, Sage. I'm Bryson."

A wall of silence stood between them.

"I think I've seen you here and there, but we've never really talked," Sage mentioned.

"Yeah, probably at one of Gabriel's birthday parties," Bryson removed his hand from the casket. "Me and Autumn didn't really speak much," Bryson added.

Sage didn't know what to say, so she kept quiet.

"I just wanna thank you and the other ladies for showing up. My mama really appreciated ya'll," Bryson added.

"Autumn was like family to me," Sage responded. "I wouldn't miss this day for the world."

Bryson looked over at her.

"She died so young. She had her whole life ahead of her. I just... I just don't understand why God would let this fuckin' happen," Bryson said. "I don't understand it either," Sage agreed. "She was... she was amazing."

Bryson stuffed his hands into his pants pocket.

"There was this one time when we were jits," Bryson began, a soft smile gracing his lips as he stared off into the distance, lost in the memory. "Me and Autumn were maybe thirteen and sixteen. It was summer, brutally hot, like always, but we ain't care. We snuck out late one night, determined to make it to this hidden swimming hole we'd heard about. It was a bop. Way out past the old citrus groves, miles away from everythin'."

He paused, chuckling lightly. "We wasn't even prepared. We had no maps because our phones were dead. Just an idea of where to go. We ended up getting completely lost. It was pitch black, the only light coming from the moon and the fireflies. I remember Autumn was spooked. Every rustle in the bushes, every owl hoot, she'd jump. I tried to act all hard and shit, like I knew exactly where we were going, but inside I was just as scared as she was."

Bryson's expression softened, a hint of sadness entering his eyes. "We stumbled around for hours, scratched up by thorns, covered in mosquito bites. We were both on the verge of tears when we heard running water. We followed the sound, and then, there it was. This beautiful little waterfall, falling into a crystal-clear pool. Not gon lie, It was magical."

He closed his eyes for a moment, reliving the memory. "We ain't even hesitate. We stripped down to our underwear and jumped in. The water was cold as fuck, it took our breath away, but it was the most refreshing thing I'd ever felt. We stayed there for hours, just talking, laughing, and splashing each other. We talked about everything – our dreams, our fears, our hopes for the future. It was one of the few times we really connected, truly felt like brother and sister."

"And now," Bryson continued, his voice barely a whisper. "Jit gone. Taken from me."

He opened his eyes, the cemetery blurring through a fresh film of tears. The silence that settled between them felt as vast and empty as the hole in his chest. He stood there for a long moment. Every fiber of his being screamed to escape this place.

"I think it's better off I get going," Bryson suggested. He took a deep breath, squared his shoulders, and turned to walk away from the casket.

"Wait. You think they gonna figure out who did it?" projected Sage.

Bryson didn't reply, he just kept walking.

When Bryson got to the car Mrs. Hayes was in the passenger seat while Gabriel was playing with a toy in the back. Bryson could see the tears trickling down her cheek. She uncrossed her arms to open the door for him. He slid in the driver's side.

Bryson buckled his seatbelt, the click too loud in the hush of grief. He glanced at his mother's swollen eyes, rimmed red from days of tears.

"Mom," he murmured.

She turned to him. "Oh, Bryson..." Her voice was small.

He squeezed her hand. "We're gonna find who did this, Ma. I swear it."

She nodded, pressing her palm over his. "We will, mijo. We will."

He put the car in drive and pulled away from the curb, leaving the cemetery.

As Bryson drove, Mrs. Hayes stared out the window, her mind replaying a memory: Autumn as a little girl, dancing in their small apartment, her dress a blur of color, her laughter echoing through the rooms. Mrs. Hayes had often worried about her daughter, about the dangers of the world, about the darkness that seemed to lurk at the edges of their lives. She had tried to shield her, to protect her, but ultimately, she had failed. *I should have seen it*, she thought. *I should have known. Was it the things I did or didn't do? Was I not enough?* The weight of this perceived failure pressed down on her, heavier than any physical burden, and for a moment, she felt as though she might shatter into a million pieces.

Chapter 6- Sage

Sage woke as dusk was settling, remembering she had work to do. She rolled over in her bed but then she heard a knock on the front door. She checked her cellphone sitting on the nightstand. It was forty-five minutes past six. After the funeral ended at noon, she came home and cried to sleep. Her body felt like it was hit by an eighteen-wheeler.

Another knock rattled the front door. At first gently, then fists slammed like drums. She hadn't ordered anything. It wasn't Amazon. It couldn't be the detectives. Her stomach twisted.

Him. The thought hit her chest like a hammer. Autumn's killer. Coming for her next. Sage didn't know what to do. She got onto her feet.

I could sneak out onto the balcony and jump three stories down into the dumpster.

The thought flashed in her head even though she knew there was a possibility she wouldn't survive. She stumbled into sweatpants, padded into the kitchen, yanked open the drawer. Her hand wrapped around a kitchen knife. She crept to the door and squinted through the peephole.

A muscular man was standing by the staircase with a bouquet of white tulips limp in his hands. His black T-shirt spelled out *Led Zeppelin* across the front and his head was covered with a mustard-colored beanie. Sage opened the door.

"Whatchu want, Arlo?"

"I wantchu back, Sage-Marie." His voice was syrup-sweet and full of stale promises.

Sage rolled her eyes. She didn't want him back. Their toxic relationship had ended. Autumn had hated him. *You deserve better*, Autumn used to say, as she handed Sage ice packs for her black eye.

"It's over. I'm done. I'm no longer in love with you. I'm choosing myself this time. I got too much going on right now. Y'know Autumn died, right? The funeral was today."

"I know," He lifted the sad flowers like a peace treaty. "I heard, that's why I brought you some flowers.

I'm sorry about your friend, I really am, but things don't gotta go this way between us. I promise I won't put my hands on you ever again. I'm such a scumbag for giving you a black eye," Arlo said. A smirk twisted his lying lips, his long brown hair covering one side of his face.

Sage leaned against the doorframe. She folded her arms.

"Take your flowers and shove them up your ass, Arlo," Sage snapped.

Arlo's grin curdled. He stepped closer, crowding the doorway.

"I came over being nice. You gonna take it there? I promise you don't want that."

Sage didn't flinch. She shifted, blade glinting.

"You gonna hit me again? You gonna force me to stay again?" Her voice didn't shake. Not anymore.

"Wow, I should be happy and forget about everything you did because you brought some lousy, beat up $5 tulips? What would I do without you Prince Charming?"

"You think you're tough now, huh? Fuck you, Sage. You know, you ain't nothin' but trailer trash. Been trailer trash just like your whole family. That's why your father was a—," Arlo didn't get to finish his thoughts. Sage was right up on him in a heartbeat. She pressed the knife up against his stomach. Arlo dropped the bouquet of tulips to the floor.

"That's why my father was a what? Go ahead. Let me hear you say it. I double dog dare you. Finish that sentence. I dare you. I'll gut you right here, let your balls roll around like loose change," threatened Sage.

Arlo's eyes flicked from her face to the knife. "Al...alright...alright I gotchu," Arlo wheezed.

"My best friend aint even been dead 48 hours and here you come with the bullshit. You really bring the worst outta me. All this time I let you treat me like crap. It stops today. I'm sick and tired. So, go ahead. Say it big man," Sage said. Her voice projected through the hallway of the apartment building.

"I'm sorry about Autumn. I'll leave you alone. I'm sorry," Arlo pleaded.

Sage looked him over. She really wanted to reciprocate all the damage he had done to her. Let him get a dose of his own medicine but everything that was boiling inside of her cooled down in an instant. He was just a scared little boy, likely shaped by witnessing his mother's domestic abuse, and unable to break the cycle.

"You better be sorry. And pick up your sorry-ass flowers while you're at it and don't come back to my fucking house."

She stepped back and removed the knife from his stomach. Arlo took off down the staircase without picking up the tulips. When he got to the first floor. He finally looked back.

"Fuck you, Sage! You'll regret this!"

"Go away, asshole," Sage said. It came out flat. She stepped into her apartment.

"Coward," she murmured, shutting the door.

Chapter 7-Sage

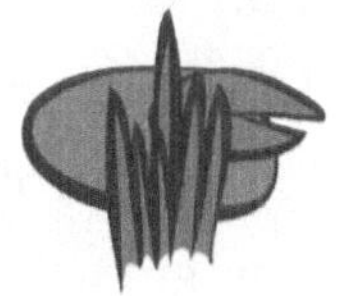

I should've done that years ago, Sage thought. *Autumn would've been proud of me.* Her hands shook as she set the knife in the sink. She'd spent years shrinking, apologizing—but not anymore. As she looked up, her eyes met with Autumn's bedroom door.

The once-bright yellow paint on Autumn's door was peeling, exposing bare wood beneath. Autumn had always wanted to repaint it.

What was the point of painting it now, thought Sage.

Sage made her way to the bathroom and removed her clothes. Steam curled off her shoulders as she stood under the shower's lukewarm stream. Water cascading down her back in thin, warm sheets. She pressed her forehead to the tile, eyes squeezed shut, breath fogging the glass door. Her skin had pruned long ago, but she couldn't bring herself to turn off the water. It was the only place that muffled her thoughts. The only place where she could let her shoulders fall away from her ears.

She turned off the water and stepped out of the bathtub. She stood for a moment, staring at her reflection in the foggy mirror. She wiped it with her hand and looked at the girl staring back at her. She didn't look like herself. Pale. Hollow-eyed. Bruised in ways that didn't show up on skin.

She ran a towel through her hair, walked to her room, and opened the drawer that still held Autumn's things. There wasn't much. A spare toothbrush, a bottle of perfume with a cracked cap, and a small, leather-bound journal. Sage had opened it once before and read just a few words before slamming it shut, afraid of what it might tell her. Today, she opened it again.

The first entry was dated just about a year to date.
September 7, 2018
Someone followed me again today. I don't know if I'm being paranoid or if it's real. But I know what fear feels like. It smells like mold and tastes like blood in the back of my throat. I don't want to scare Sage, so I haven't told her. Not yet.

Sage closed the journal gently and placed it back in the drawer. She sat on the bed and stared at the floor for a long time. Her fingers itched to text Bryson. To call the detectives. To do something. But she was tired of waiting for other people to save her. Autumn hadn't waited. Autumn had faced whatever it was alone.

She stretched out across the sofa in the living room. Her body stuck to the faux leather. Something caught her attention across the room. On the wall, a framed photo captured her and Autumn's bright smiles from the day they moved in together. They were hugging each other while sitting on a red bench in front of a movie theater. Autumn wore a yellow shirt in the picture. Sage wore overalls and black boots. Her hair, as brown as a cup of hot chocolate, fell to her shoulders.

Sage reminisced on the moment. Moving out of her mothers' house had been terrifying, but having Autumn by her side made the transition easy. If she looked closely, she could see a bruise over her left eye. A keepsake she'd received arguing with Arlo. The girl in the picture had been insecure and weak, always trying to please others and never knowing her worth. If Arlo had shown up with flowers, then, she would have accepted them and mistaken it for love. Then Arlo would've continued the same abusive cycle.

Autumn was different. Confident and self-assured, she didn't take crap from anyone. Sage had always wanted to be fierce and courageous like her. Tears welled in her eyes, and she looked away from the picture, blotting them with the corner of her t-shirt. She rested the back of her neck on the armrest. Feeling the cracks in the sofa pressing against her skin.

"Dang. My girl really gone," Sage muttered, staring at the ceiling.

She had a flashback of her and Autumn.

***

They were in Ft. Lauderdale. The sun, warm and golden. Autumn, wearing her favorite bright yellow t-shirt and cutoff shorts. She was attempting to teach Sage how to ride a skateboard.

"Come on, Sage! Just lean into it!" Autumn yelled, her laughter echoing through the park.

Sage wobbled on the board, her arms flailing wildly as she tried to keep her balance. "I'm going to fall! I know I'm going to fall!"

"You're not gonna fall! I'm right here!" Autumn called with optimism.

Sure enough, Sage's foot slipped, and she went tumbling to the ground with a loud "Oof!"

Autumn rushed over, her laughter fading into concern. "Oh, Sage! Are you okay?"

Sage sat up, brushing the dirt off her jeans. "Yeah, I'm fine. Just... maybe skateboarding isn't my thing."

Autumn grinned, offering her a hand up. "Don't be ridiculous! Everyone falls the first few times. It's part of the process. Here, try again."

Sage hesitated, looking at the skateboard with suspicion. "I don't know..."

"Come on! I promise I won't let you fall this time," Autumn said, her eyes sparkling with determination.

Sage sighed, but she couldn't resist Autumn's infectious enthusiasm. She climbed back onto the board, and Autumn patiently guided her, her hands steady on Sage's shoulders.

"See? You got this! You're a natural!" Autumn said, even though Sage was barely moving.

"A natural disaster, maybe," Sage muttered, but a small smile tugged at the corner of her lips.

After a while, Sage started to get the hang of it, wobbling down the path, Autumn cheering her on every step of the way.

"You're doing it! I knew you could!" Autumn exclaimed, jumping up and down.

Sage grinned, feeling a surge of triumph. She did it.

"I did it!" she yelled, laughing. "I actually did it!"

And then, she hit a small rock, and the skateboard went flying out from under her. She landed in a heap of leaves, the wind knocked out of her.

Autumn rushed over, her face a mask of concern. "Sage! Oh my god, are you okay?!"

Sage lay there for the moment, then burst out laughing. "I think so," she said, still chuckling. "I just... I think I'm done with skateboarding for today."

Autumn laughed too, relief flooding her face. "Yeah, me too," she said, sitting down beside Sage. "Let's just... enjoy the sun for a while. And maybe get some ice cream."

They sat there for a long time, talking about everything and nothing, the sun warm on their skin, the sound of children playing in the distance. Autumn told her one of the wild stories she made up in her head of saving the world and defeating bad guys. And Sage just listened, content to be in her presence, amazed at her imagination. It was one of those perfect days.

Sage blinked, the memory fading, leaving behind a sharp ache in her chest. She closed her eyes, picturing Autumn's bright smile, her infectious laughter, her unwavering belief in her. Autumn had been so full of life, so full of dreams. She had wanted to make a difference, to change the world, to make it a better place. And now she was dead.

Sage knew then that she couldn't just walk away. She couldn't let Autumn's death be in vain. She had to do something. Something more. She thought of what Autumn would have wanted, what Autumn would have done. She would have fought. She would have stood up for what was right. She would have made sure that the killer, and everyone else involved, paid for what they had done.

Sage stood up. She knew what she had to do. As she walked to her room, Autumn's voice filled her ears. *Don't let them get away with this, Sage. Please. Promise me.*

And Sage whispered to herself, to the memory of her best friend, "*I promise, Autumn. I promise.*" It wasn't just a whisper; it was a vow, a burden she willingly took on. But where to start?

The room felt small. She paced, her mind a whirlwind of fragmented thoughts. She grabbed a worn notebook and a pen, her hands trembling slightly. On the first page, she wrote: *Autumn.* Below it, a list: *Black Eye. Big Cypress Swamp. Secrets.* It felt inadequate, childish even, but it was something.

Chapter 8- Sterling

President Sterling reached for the phone, his hand trembling. The crystal decanter on his desk seemed to mock him, its amber whiskey, a symbol of the control he was rapidly losing. He punched in a number, fumbling the buttons like a drunk. It rang twice before a gruff voice answered.

"Yeah?"

"It's Sterling," President Sterling said, his voice tight with barely suppressed panic. "We have a problem."

"What kind of problem?" The man on the other end was monotonous, empty of warmth.

"The dead girl's boyfriend," Sterling spat, lowering his voice, glancing nervously at the closed office door.

"He knows too much."

A low chuckle came from the other end. "He ain't gonna do nothin'."

"That's what you said about the girl," Sterling retorted, his fear momentarily overridden by anger. "You promised it would be clean—quiet. Now look at us."

"Hey, things happen," the voice said, a hint of annoyance creeping in. "The swamp ain't predictable. But we handled it. The girl's gone. That's what you wanted, right?"

Sterling's jaw clenched so tight his teeth ached." I wanted the problem solved," forced Sterling, behind his closed teeth. "Not replaced with a bigger one. Now the police are involved. And this boyfriend... he's walking roun' with too much information."

There was a pause on the other end.

"Alright, alright. Don't get your panties in a bunch. We'll handle it. Just tell us what you want."

"I want him stopped," Sterling insisted, his voice pleading now. "Make him go away."

"Go away?" the voice repeated, a dangerous edge to it. "Like the other one?"

Sterling's blood ran cold. He hadn't meant... not like that. Not another death. But the thought, once planted, took root. He was desperate. His reputation, his career, everything he had built was on the line. He couldn't afford to have this boy, Autumn's boyfriend, unraveling everything.

"Just... make him understand," Sterling said, choosing his words carefully. "Make him understand that this is none of his business. That the swamp keeps its secrets. Let him know that swamp water rises for those who stir the mud."

"Got it," the voice said. "Consider it handled. But it's gonna cost you extra. Loose ends ain't cheap."

Sterling swallowed the taste of bile in his mouth. "Just... make it go away."

He hung up the phone, his hand still trembling. He had just sanctioned... what? He didn't want to think about it. He just wanted this nightmare to be over. He looked at the portraits on the wall, the stern-faced men who had held power before him. Had they faced such moments of desperation? Had they made such choices? He didn't know. But he knew one thing. The swamp was a dangerous place, not just for those who ventured into its depths, but for those who hid secrets there. And he was now waist-deep in its murky water. He had to protect his interests, his reputation, his carefully constructed world. He poured another glass, throat burning as the whiskey slid down. *Anyone*, he thought. *Anyone who tries to ruin me will sink with her.*

Chapter 9- Bryson

Bryson sat in the den sipping on some coffee, the rich aroma a comforting counterpoint to the storm brewing outside. The wind howled, rattling the windows as rain lashed against the glass. He grabbed a bottle of tequila from the table and poured a double shot into his coffee.

He downed the drink. The burn worked its way down his throat, spreading a warmth that didn't reach his chest. He thought about another shot. Instead, he filled the water glass and drained it in two gulps. Booze wouldn't fix this. He needed the pain more than the numbness.

Bryson held the empty mug to his right thigh before setting it down with a thud. He glanced at the rain-streaked window, the world outside a blur of gray. His thoughts drifted back to Autumn, and guilt washed over him. He remembered her last birthday, how he'd promised to take her out, but then bailed at the last minute. Claiming he was too tired from a job he hated. Another excuse. He pictured Autumn's face, not the one from the morgue, but the one from their childhood, scraped knees and missing front teeth, her eyes wide with adoration for her big brother. He'd been her protector then, a role he'd abandoned somewhere along the way.

He remembered the time she'd found his stash of stolen hubcaps in the shed. Instead of ratting him out, she'd just looked at him with a silent plea, a look that said, "Why, Bryson?" He'd shrugged it off, the king of cool, but her disappointment had stung more than any lecture from their momma. That was Autumn – quiet strength, unwavering loyalty, and a look that could see right through his tough guy facade.

They'd drifted apart slowly, like two boats on a lazy river, the current pulling them in different directions. He'd gotten tangled in the reeds of the swamp, in the murky waters of easy money and bad decisions. She'd stayed closer to the shore, her dreams as bright as the rising sun on the horizon over the water. He'd always assumed there would be time to bridge the gap, to pull his boat back to hers. Time, the one thing death stole without a warning. He always thought he'd pass away before his baby sister. He considered himself the *bad one.*

He wasn't the good one, not by a long shot. Autumn was. And now she was gone, leaving him adrift in a sea of his own making. He raised the empty mug again, not for another shot, but as a silent toast to the sister he'd failed. The sister who deserved so much more than a B-Day text and a broken promise. He'd seen the disappointment flicker in her eyes on Facetime, the way her smile had faltered for just a moment. Now, he'd give anything to take that moment back, to have one more conversation, one more shared laugh. One more anything. If he'd taken her out for her birthday maybe that would've changed everything. Maybe it would've brought them closer. Maybe she'd still be alive.

He let out a sigh. It was all just a bunch of what ifs. She was supposed to be the one to bury him. But when death comes knocking it claims anyone in its path, no matter how young, old, beautiful or kind. The old adage *'the good die young'* seemed a stark reality to him.

He sat back on the sofa. The sofa was a gift from his mama after he got out of prison. A place he'd rest his feet after lifting patients and wiping their asses for twelve hours straight.

His hand reached out, grasping a leather book from the seat next to him—The Bible. *The King James version.* He'd promised his mama that he would keep God in his life. She'd say God would never leave him, nor forsake him. He had read all 66 books of the Bible in prison. In those days he would cry to sleep meditating on the words. The Bible was the only thing that gave him hope. Helped him endure each day in that cold concrete box. However, he didn't pay God any mind after his release. No more prayers. No devotions.

Now, he figured he needed God again. Times were tough. It was time to pick his Bible back up. He felt ashamed. His mama always told him that God wanted to maintain a relationship with him, even during the good times too. He tussled with the thoughts of why he needed God or the Bible when things were going good.

He recited the commandments under his breath. *Thou shalt have no other gods before me. Thou shalt not steal. Thou shalt not kill.*

Before he could open the book his phone vibrated on the side table. He checked the number. It was detective Mason.

"Hello," Bryson answered.

"Hello, Mr. Hayes, this is Detective Mason. How are things going?"

"I just saw my sister get put in the ground. Whatchu think?"

Mason paused.

"Sorry, Mr. Hayes. Stupid question. We are doing everything we can to find the suspect. But we need more, would it be okay if we came by to speak with you and your mother?"

"I really don't fuck with twelve," he rubbed his temples, the events of the past few days weighing heavily on him. "Even when y'all try to help," he continued, the *y'all* coming out with a bit of a Southern drawl. "It always feels like shit ends up going sideways. The last thing, the absolute last thing, I want is my mama losing both of her kids in the same damn week," Bryson said. Mason sighed.

"I understand," said Mason. He shifted slightly. His badge felt heavier than usual.

"But do you really?" asked Bryson, the question loaded with unspoken history. "Do you understand what it's like to see blue lights in your rearview and feel your heart jump into your throat, even when you know you ain't done nothin' wrong? Do you understand what it's like to have to teach your little cousins and young Black homies how to act around cops, so they don't end up on a t-shirt or locked up?"

"Do I?" Mason repeated, his voice taking on a deeper, more resonant tone. "Mr. Hayes, I am a Black man first, and a cop right after that. I grew up in this city. I know the streets, the stories, the fears. I understand the pain of being looked at sideways. That's why I decided to become a cop. Not to be a part of the problem, but to be a part of the solution. So, I can protect my community, so I can treat *us* fairly, so maybe, just maybe, things can be different. For my kids, for your family, for everyone."

"Yeah... yeah, I get that. I really do. It ain't easy, is it? For either of us. You trying to do right, and... well, you know how it is for us. I hope you can make a difference, man. I really do," said Bryson.

"Thank you, Mr. Hayes. I appreciate that. And I understand your hesitation. But I need your help with this. Any little detail you can remember about Autumn's life, her friends, her acquaintances, anything that seemed off... it could make a difference in finding who did this. Do you know of anyone?"

"Nah, not really... we weren't as close as we could've been, so I don't think there's anything I'm gonna be able to help you with," Bryson said.

"What about your mom, Mr. Hayes?"

"To be honest my mama ain't ready for all this bruh," said Bryson.

"Mr. Hayes, I know this is hard but—"

"Wait, did somebody beat the shit outta yo' lil' sister, throw her in a swamp then watch as she gets devoured by a gator?" Bryson said. His grip latched around the phone.

"No, but uhm—"

"Mane, I gotta go detective," Bryson said. He cut the phone off and placed it back on the side table, the click of the disconnected call echoing in the sudden silence of the room. He sat there; the warmth of the phone still in his hand.

Finally, he rose and walked over to the bookcase, his eyes scanning the spines, not really seeing them. He was replaying the conversation with Mason in his head, the detective's questions, his own answers. He picked up a framed photograph, one of the four of them: Autumn, his mama, his father—who was recovering from a stroke at the time—and himself. Another picture of Bryson, Autumn and Gabriel the day Bryson was released from prison. It was the first time Bryson held Gabriel. Bryson picked up the picture and blew the dust from the frame. He ran his fingers along the edge before putting it back on the bookcase. He walked through the living room and into the chocolate room. He flicked the light on, and the space bloomed with a warm, amber glow. Everything in the room was a shade of brown, from the deep mahogany bookshelves lining one wall to the plush, caramel-colored rug that muffled his footsteps. The velvet textured curtains, heavy and dark, were drawn, blocking out the sun. They created a sense of enclosure, a private sanctuary from the world outside. The air was filled with an earthy, citrusy fragrance that always calmed him. It mingled with the faintest hint of old paper and something indefinably "him"—a blend of sweat, laundry detergent, and the subtle scent of his own skin.

A small, worn armchair sat in one corner, draped with a brown throw blanket and scattered with a few well-loved paperbacks. A low coffee table, also a rich chocolate hue, held a stack of art and sport books and a small, intricate wooden puzzle box that he sometimes fiddled with when he was thinking. A vintage record player occupied a place of honor on a small, antique cabinet, surrounded by a carefully curated collection of jazz and blues records he got from his father. The walls were adorned with framed posters, mostly of musicians and athletes, in tones of sepia and brown, further emphasizing the room's monochromatic palette.

This room wasn't just a place; it was an extension of himself. A space for introspection, for finding solace, for escaping the noise and chaos that sometimes threatened to overwhelm him. It was his space to break without being seen.

Bryson fell to the floor, the worn carpet cushioning his hands as he began doing pushups. Each movement was a sharp, controlled burst of effort, punctuated by the hiss of his breath.

It reshaped him within the cold confines of prison. Prison had taught him this discipline, forged him from someone slight into someone strong. He could feel the burn in his muscles, a physical manifestation of the pain and transformation he'd endured.

The movements reminded him of his father from long ago. He pictured his daddy in their backyard, muscles straining as he did push-ups, sit-ups, and pull-ups on the rusty bar he'd welded himself. His father used to push him to join in. Back then, Bryson had scoffed, more interested in the flickering screen of a video game than physical exertion. Now, he understood. These exercises were more than just building strength; they were a release, a way to grapple with the stress and turmoil that churned within him. Each rep was a small victory, a step towards control and self-mastery.

Bryson had no son of his own to pass down the lessons his father had instilled, but he had Gabriel—his sister's little boy—who now looked to him for guidance. The weight of responsibility settled heavy on his shoulders; he had to be a pillar of strength for Gabriel, especially now. The thought of Bryson's mama not being in his life, a world without her unwavering love and prayers, sent a shiver down Bryson's spine. His nephew would never experience such a love. Gabriel, barely old enough to understand the permanence of loss, was now without his mother. Tears welled in his eyes, blurring his vision, and fell silently, leaving dark spots on the carpet. Tears for who they were and what they all had lost.

Chapter 10- Sage & Bryson

Sage checked her phone. Ten minutes to nine. Early, but not so early she'd be rude knocking on a door. *Bryson had to be awake by now*, she told herself.

Sage was certain this was Bryson's house. She double-checked the address—same one from the package he'd mailed Autumn last Christmas. She'd never been here in person. The house was a faded green, single-story, a neat patch of grass ringed by scraggly palm trees. The mailbox leaned, dented, but still standing.

Sage eased her car, a beat-up Honda Civic, to the curb, the tires brushing against the concrete. She killed the engine. For a moment, she just sat there, gathering her courage, her fingers drumming nervously on the steering wheel. Then, she reached over and turned up the volume on the stereo. A familiar song filled the car. It was one of Autumn's favorites. She closed her eyes; each note a bittersweet reminder of her lost friend. The song, *Waterfalls* by TLC, a tune they'd often sung together at the top of their lungs during late-night drives. Autumn had always belted out Chillis' lines with a joyful abandon, her voice a little off-key but full of heart. Now, the music felt like a tender ache. Taking a deep breath, she opened her eyes and reached for the door handle.

As she stepped onto the walkway, the front door swung open. Bryson stepped out, keys in hand, head down.

"Hey, Bryson." Her voice cracked a little.

Bryson flinched. The keys hit the porch with a clatter. "Sage, right?" He scooped them up, rubbing his neck.

"Sorry—didn't mean to startle you. Got a minute? I just... need to talk."

Bryson shifted his weight, eyed the sky. "Got a run to get in before the heat, but yeah. C'mon in."

She followed him through the door.

"You ever think about getting those rainbow sunglasses the runners wear? Oakleys, right?" she asked, nervous chatter spilling out.

"Yeah—nah. I'm good," responded Bryson.

The smell of bergamot hung around her as she followed Bryson into the kitchen. Sage sat, pushed her hair behind her ears.

"Today makes it a month," she said. Bryson crossed his arms as he braced against the kitchen counter.

"Yeah. I know," Bryson looked over at the refrigerator. "You want some water?"

"I'm good. How ya been? Since I saw you at the funeral? "Sage asked.

He shrugged. "Survivin'. Ain't much else to do."

"You hear anything from the cops?" asked Sage.

Bryson responded. "They called. Nothing since. Probably done what they gonna do."

"I went to the station. Asked for Mason, Monroe. They told me the case is on hold. No leads. Nobody talking," said Sage.

She edged forward on the chair.

"Life ain't been sunny since, Bryson. I go to school, work, then back home. That's about it. Most days I don't even want to eat. I walk by her bedroom door every morning and lose my appetite," Sage said.

She took a deep breath. "I don't know about you, but I can't sleep another night knowing this."

Bryson didn't say a word. Sage looked down at her feet.

"I see her in my dreams, Bryson. Her body split into two halves. Everything inside of her falling out. Both halves floating in a big ocean of red. Blood everywhere."

"Stop!" His voice cracked like old wood. She stopped.

"Sorry, Bryson. I just keep thinking about what happened when she died. I can't believe the cops still ain't found nothing yet," Sage said.

"I ain't surprised that twelve stopped looking. They don't give a fuck about a little Spanish girl being dead anyways. We live in racist ass America. It's just like those days when they used to hang my people from them poplar trees. It was a celebration for them. Guess what? They still lynching," Bryson said.

"That's exactly why we can't let it go. If they're not going to find justice for Autumn, then we must. We can't just sit here and let her death be in vain. There's gotta be something we can do. That's why I wanted to talk to you," Sage said.

"Whatchu want to talk about?" Bryson asked. Sage shifted her body in the chair. She'd been waiting for this moment for a week. She was hesitant but she couldn't hold back.

"I don't have a perfect plan or anything. But I was thinking... did Autumn ever mention anyone she was afraid of? Or anyone who was bothering her? Anything at all? Maybe we can put our heads together and figure out where to start. Even the smallest detail might be helpful," Sage suggested, letting out everything so fast that she forgot to take a breath. Bryson unfolded his arms.

"Hol' up, you want us to play like we some detectives and shit?" chuckled Bryson.

"Call it what you want but you her fucking blood, man. If someone had done this to my lil' sister, this world would not fucking sleep until I found out who did it. There's a coward walking around right now thinking he got away with this shit. He's sleeping like a baby, doing whatever he fucking wants. He killed our sister. That's what Autumn was to me, my sister. He fed her to the gator like bait. Then that son of bitch stood and watched her take her last breath. I don't know about you, but I can't live with myself knowing that he's still free and breathing. You good with that?" Sage said.

"Look, I get it, Sage. I'm hurting too. But you know I can't... I can't get caught up in anythin' that might look wrong. I just got my life back on track. I already lost two years of it in prison. My record ain't clean, and I ain't trying to go back to that life. I can't be out here looking for trouble. I came out and I ain't tryna look back. Look around here. I'm a LPN making decent money. I bought my first house. I gotta look over Gabriel because Autumn is dead and his father is a dead beat. I got my mama counting on me to stay out of trouble. I got responsibilities. I understand your anger but playing detective... that's dangerous. I ain't going for it. I just can't," Bryson said.

Sage twisted her hair around her middle finger.

"So, you just gonna be a pussy? It's cool, me and my brother will handle it."

Bryson's eyebrows crumbled up.

"First off, watch your fuckin' mouth in my house woe. You think I don't want this man dead? I had to bury my lil' sister, my only sister. I couldn't even tell it was her; her face was all messed up. My mama cries every time we get on the phone. I look at her son and realize that he'll never know his mama. I blame myself every fuckin' day, from when I wake up to when I go to bed. I met you one fucking time and now you talkin' all crazy. You don't know shit about me, girl. What, you thought I would crash out because you had this grand idea?"

Red flared in Bryson's eyes, and he trembled. Sage saw it all. She stood up.

"I thought you had balls, man," Sage said.

"Get outta my house," Bryson bellowed. Sage walked toward the door, then stopped.

"I just... I miss her so much. And it feels like no one cares. Like her life didn't matter. And I thought... I thought maybe you felt the same. And maybe we could do something about it. But I guess not. I'm just... I'm so lost right now. I shouldn't have talked to you like that, especially in your house. I'm sorry, Bryson. Just... think about it, okay?"

She stepped out and closed the door.

His phone buzzed—Sage's shape shrinking on the tiny screen, her anger echoing off the pavement.

He took a seat on the sofa. His chest rose and fell in short, shallow movements. He grabbed a pillow and slung it across the room. It hit the entertainment center and plopped onto the floor. He slammed his fists into the sofa.

That little white girl had the audacity to sit there and tell him he didn't have the balls. He shot up from the sofa and made his way through the front door. He stood in the middle of the driveway, running in place trying to let some steam off.

Did Sage really think she was the only one who wanted justice? There wasn't a day that he wasn't thinking about Autumn. Any moment he wasn't thinking about her he felt guilty. Some days were a little easier and others were arduous. On hard days, he'd spend his lunch break in the car, replaying Autumn's voicemails. Her voice and words were so familiar, they were like a song he knew by heart.

He should've just told her to leave as soon as she showed up. He could have confessed his violent fantasies—the hot lead between the killer's eyes, the gruesome image of the man chopped into pieces.

His mind flashed back to a sweltering afternoon at Blue Onion State Penitentiary. The tension in the air, and the clang of metal echoed in the distance. He'd been cornered, a target because of his quiet nature. But he learned quickly. He'd transformed, becoming someone else entirely. He remembered the look in the other guy's eyes, the moment the fear set in, the moment Bryson showed him what he was truly capable of. Now, the memory felt like a lifetime ago, a chapter he desperately wanted to keep closed.

He didn't want to go back to what he was, a man who thrived in that brutal world. Every achievement had been hard-won; he'd worked relentlessly to become a nurse and to make Mrs. Hayes proud. This was his life now. A life dedicated to healing, to caring for others. A world away from the cold, concrete walls and the constant threat of violence. He didn't want to go back to what he was, the person who had thrown it all away, who had embraced the darkness and nearly lost himself within. The two years he'd spent in prison for a crime he swore he didn't commit—a bar fight gone wrong, where he'd been wrongly accused and convicted of aggravated assault. The injustice of it all still burned in his gut, a constant reminder of how easily his life could be derailed.

He glanced at his hands, the same hands that skillfully inserted IVs and gently bathed patients, hands that had once clenched into fists ready to strike, ready to defend. He thought of Gabriel, and the innocent way he looked at the world. He couldn't let that innocence be shattered by the same violence that had stained his own past. He had to be better. He owed that to Gabriel. He owed it to his mama and Autumn.

He was trapped between two worlds: the one he'd clawed his way into, a world of order and healing, and the one he desperately wanted to leave behind, a world of chaos and violence. The urge to hunt down Autumn's killer, to deliver justice himself, was a primal scream within him. But the fear of what that would unleash, the fear of losing everything he'd fought for, held him back like an anchor.

He walked back into the house. He knew he couldn't stay like this. He couldn't live with the guilt, the anger, the helplessness. He had to do something. But what? How could he reconcile the need for justice with the life he'd built? The life he had sacrificed so much for.

He walked into the chocolate room. He found himself at the bookcase, his hand hovering over the framed photo of Autumn, Gabriel, and himself. He picked up the photo, his thumb gently brushing over Autumn's smiling face. He closed his eyes and made a silent promise. *I won't let you down, sis. I swear I'll figure this out. For you. For Momma. For Gabriel.* With a sigh, he set the framed picture back on the shelf. His eyes, lingering for a moment, carefully drifted to the rows of books lining the shelf beneath. A title caught his eye. He hadn't read it in years. It was a book on criminal psychology. He picked it up. Maybe, just maybe, there was another way. A way that didn't involve returning to the violence that haunted him, but a way that still led to justice for Autumn. He opened the book to the first page. A small, worn bookmark fell to the floor. He picked it up. A small piece of paper with a quote written on it in his father's handwriting: *The mind is a weapon. Use it wisely.* Bryson stared at the words. A flicker of something sparked in his eyes.

Chapter 11- Bugsy

Bugsy hauled up the living room blinds, and the morning sun slammed into his skull. The world outside shimmered, the grass and trees bathed in a raw, copper light. He squinted, pushing through the glare, his boots crunching on the parched earth as he trudged toward the shed. The heat pressed down on him, a thick, suffocating blanket.

Bugsy swung the shed door open. He slipped his headphones over his bald head. His hand was covered in sawdust. He'd been cutting baseboards for the nursery—Janine was six months along, finally showing, finally real. A girl, they'd learned last week. Probably the only good thing he'd ever make. Sweat from his skin lathered the earmuffs. He was about to grab a miter saw to cut a slab of wood when Janine ran out the back door.

"Your cell phone is ringing. Y'know, the old Nokia," she said. Bugsy pulled off his headphones.

"Go grab it."

"You're always so secretive about that stupid thing."

"Lady, would you go get me the fuckin' phone," Bugsy said. Janine folded her arms and stood in the doorway.

"How bout' you go get it yourself, you asshole. I'm not your dog, go fetch your own doggone phone."

"You don't do jack-shit around here. Move, get outta my fuckin' way," said Bugsy as he pushed past Janine.

Janine shoved her middle finger in his face.

"I can't wait to get the fuck outta here?" said Janine.

"A job would work for starters," chuckled Bugsy, as he made his way in the house.

Janine wasn't going anywhere. Bugsy knew it. She'd talked about getting a job and moving out for years. It never happened because she was taught that a man was supposed to take care of her. And that's what Bugsy did. It didn't matter how he treated her, as long as she was taken care of.

Bugsy flipped open the Nokia. He saw the missed call and knew the number. He paused a few seconds before returning the call.

"Hello?" said Bugsy, as the person picked up the phone.

"Hello. I think you know why I'm calling. I thought you were dodging me."

"Nahh, I'm not good at dodging. I sucked at dodgeball in high school," Bugsy forced out a chuckle. The man on the other end didn't seem pleased by his corny joke.

"If you don't come through, Bugsy, you know what happens. I have ways of making sure you do."

"It's been a month. We've been looking all over for him. I had a few of the fellas show up to his job but they ain't seen him. Even put a bounty on his head. That sucka probably left town. After what happened to his girl, he's definitely spooked. You should be good," Bugsy said. The man didn't say a word for about thirty seconds. When he spoke again his tone was authoritative.

"That's not enough. I want to make certain that he keeps his chops shut."

Bugsy watched a wasp build its nest under the shed's eave, patient and methodical, building something that would last. "Crap. You're really serious about this?" Bugsy asked.

"You dang right I'm serious. I don't play games; that's for little boys. I'm talking about protecting our investment. About protecting your investment."

Sterling's voice hardened. "Or did you forget who pays for that nice house you're building? Who made sure your name never came up after the girl? Anyways, we don't need him messin' things up. That's why I need you to find him. If it means going to Mars to find him then so be it."

"I don't know, man. He even left his job. He's scared for his life. I don't think he'll say anything. There's nothing to worry about."

"Listen to me, listen to me clearly. I don't give a fuck about what you think. I've been doing this for a long time. You and your people are working for me now. I'm putting food on your table. If he is not taken care of, you don't eat. As a matter of fact, you won't have a goddang mouth to eat with. I didn't want to threaten you, but you brought me here. I want us to all win. But I need that boy. You got a week."

Bugsy grinded his teeth. He placed the phone on mute to let out a shout from deep in his stomach. As he felt he was able to speak he unmuted the phone.

"I hear ya. This ain't our first rodeo. I see you talking crazy and I don't take threats lightly. Let's get that straight for the record. Me and the crew will do the best we can to find this guy because you paid me upfront. One more thing though. Just know, the same can go for you cocksucker," Bugsy said.

"I hear you tough guy. All that can be ironed out later. At this moment, I need you and your people to take care of this shit."

"Hmm. And where do you think we could find him, wise guy?"

The man didn't say anything for a few seconds.

"That girl at the swamp. Maybe you can go to her place and look around. Y'all might find something I don't know. Shoot, if I keep telling you what to do I might as well take my money back."

Bugsy laughed. It was slow in cadence and filled with a rasp.

"You really think popping up at that dead girl's house will give us the answer we need? Come on, man."

"Just my suggestion but apparently, I suck at it. That's why you're the killer and I'm not. I'll send you her address just in case."

The line went blank. Bugsy hung up the phone and put it in his pocket. "Fuckin' scumbag," he mumbled.

Bugsy stood in the doorway for a long time. The wasp kept working, adding layer after layer to its paper castle. Building something that would protect its young. Bugsy's phone buzzed. The address appeared.

He'd done terrible things for money before. Things that kept him up at night, that made him flinch

when Janine touched him unexpectedly, that he'd never
be able to wash off no matter how many houses he built
or babies he made.

One more wouldn't matter.

Chapter 12-Bryson

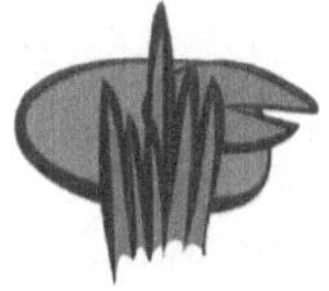

Bryson took a drag of the cigar, then sipped his coffee. Mrs. Hayes sat across from him at the table which was set in the middle of her garden. The garden was an explosion of color and life, nestled behind her quaint home. A weathered wooden gate, adorned with climbing roses, marked the entrance. Inside, winding stone pathways led through beds overflowing with a mix of carefully cultivated blooms and wild, untamed growth. Sunflowers towered over smaller flowers like cheerful sentinels, while fragrant honeysuckle climbed trellises, filling the air with a sweet perfume. A small, bubbling fountain sat in the center, attracting birds that flitted among the blossoms. In one corner, a vegetable patch thrived, with rows of tomatoes, peppers, and leafy greens.

Before Autumn's death, the garden reflected Mrs. Hayes's spirit. She would rise early, before the harshest heat of the day, and spend hours tending to her plants. Hummingbirds danced around her as she snipped dead blooms, her fingers gently coaxing life from the soil. She would chat with the roses as if they were old friends, share her worries with the sunflowers, and whisper secrets to the herbs. Gabriel would often play among the rows, his laughter mingling with the sounds of the fountain, and Autumn would sometimes join them, her hands finding their way into the soil, eager to learn her mother's ways. Now, the garden felt heavy with unspoken grief.

Mrs. Hayes had a cigarette hanging limply from her lips as she studied the plants. The smoke left a haze in the air.

"Mama, what you and Gabriel gonna do today?" Bryson asked. Mrs. Hayes didn't look at him.

"Yo no se'. The same thing we been doing for the last month. Acting like his madré isn't dead."

Bryson sipped his tea again. Maybe you can take him out to the water park. Mrs. Hayes' face crumbled.

"No water park until he knows how to swim," asserted Mrs. Hayes.

"I'm sure you'll think of something then mama."

Mrs. Hayes knocked her cigarette at the corner of the table; ash landed in the dirt. Bryson, on the other hand, used the ashtray on the table to ash his cigar.

She took a long drag off her cigarette and exhaled through her nose. "I can't seem to think clearly nowadays." The tip of the cigarette resembled a red traffic light. "I don't think they'll ever catch that cabrón," she said. Disturbed by his mother's words, Bryson put out his blunt prematurely and stuffed it into the ashtray. Her eyes became windows to a deep well of despondency—all hope lost.

He looked away, and got up from the table, the metal chair scraping against the walkway stones. Bryson was uneasy, losing the little bit of comfort his mother's garden gave him.

"Is everything okay, Brysonito?" Mrs. Hayes asked, her voice softer now, a hint of concern creeping in.

"Mama, what do you mean is 'everything ok'?

"Something is bothering you. It's in your face, son. What is it?" Mrs. Hayes asked.

Bryson sighed, running a hand through his hair. He turned back to her, the anger fading, replaced by a weary resignation.

"Autumn's friend came by my house a few days ago."

Mrs. Hayes stubbed out her cigarette. "What did she want?"

Bryson folded his arms. "She thinks we should look for who did this."

A long silence followed, interrupted by the chirping of crickets. Mrs. Hayes stared at her hands, her fingers twisting together nervously.

"And what do you think, mijo?" she finally asked, her voice barely above a whisper.

"I... I don't know," Bryson admitted, his voice laced with uncertainty. "Part of me... part of me wants to tear this whole damn city apart until I find him. But... the other part... I just... I don't want to go back to that. You know what I mean, mama?"

Mrs. Hayes nodded, her eyes filled with understanding. "I know, Brysonito. I know. But... sitting here, doing nothing... it's like we're letting them get away with it. Like we're saying Autumn's life didn't matter."

"It did matter, mama. It mattered more than anything," Bryson said fiercely. "But... I just got my life back. I can't... I can't risk losing it again."

"I understand, son. I do. But... what if...," Mrs. Hayes stopped mid-sentence.

He was waiting for his mother to tell him to leave it alone but the words never left her lips.

Bryson looked at his mother, really looked at her. He saw the pain, the grief, but he also saw the strength, the resilience that had always defined her. He knew that she wouldn't rest until justice was served, and he knew that he couldn't, in good conscience, turn his back on her.

Mrs. Hayes slowly pushed back her chair. She didn't say a word, but the weariness in her eyes spoke volumes. Her shoulders dipped, each vertebra in her spine seeming to bend under an unseen load. She pushed herself up, her hand clinging to the table before she stood. Her feet dragged softly on the paving stones as she pivoted. A hollow sound escaped her lips, like air leaking from a slow puncture, she turned and walked away, her figure fading into the shadows of the garden.

The silence she left behind weighed heavily as Bryson walked to the edge of the garden, looking out beyond the gate. He thought about Sage's visit, her passionate plea, and her words about him not having the balls. He felt a surge of anger, but it was quickly replaced by a sense of shame. She was right, in a way. He was afraid. Afraid of going back to his old life, afraid of losing everything he'd worked for.

He turned back to the house; his eyes caught the window where he knew his mother was likely inside. He knew he couldn't ignore this. He couldn't let his fear dictate his actions. He had to do something, not just for Autumn, but for his mother, for Gabriel, and for himself. He decided to go inside and talk to his mother again.

As Bryson came into the kitchen, Mrs. Hayes wasn't just staring out the window; she was watching the birds. They were so free, so light, while she felt anchored to the ground. It reminded her of an old Dominican folktale about a mother whose child was stolen by the river spirit. The mother turned into a weeping willow, forever reaching out to the water, forever mourning her loss. Was that her destiny now? To be a monument to sorrow, forever haunted by the ghost of her daughter? She turned to Bryson; her eyes filled with a mixture of pain and resolve.

"Mijo," she began, her voice trembling with emotion.

"Mama," he said softly.

She turned slowly, her eyes filled with sorrow, but there was a new glint of determination in them.

"I... I've been thinking," Bryson began. "About what you said... what you almost said."

Mrs. Hayes nodded slightly.

"Maybe... maybe Sage was right," Bryson continued. "Maybe we do need to do something."

Mrs. Hayes looked at him. "What do you have in mind, mijo?"

Bryson took a deep breath. "I don't know yet. But... We'll figure it out together."

Mrs. Hayes reached out and took his hand, squeezing it firmly. "We will," she said, her voice stronger now. "We will."

Chapter 13- Sage & Bryson

Sage approached the side of the faded, neon-lit building. The sign above, *Burger and Shake,* flickered erratically, a testament to its age. Taking a deep breath, she pushed open the heavy glass door, the bell above jingling a tinny melody that seemed to echo the nervous flutter in her stomach. The restaurant mingled scents of frying grease and the aroma of fruits. Stepping into the brightly lit burger joint, she paused, letting her eyes adjust. Booths lined the walls, the seats wore smooth with time, and a handful of patrons occupied them. Some lost in conversation, others staring absently at the vintage television mounted in the corner. Sage slowly scanned the room, she looked over at the counter where a lone waitress poured coffee, then onto the tables scattered throughout the space.

Bryson sat hunched in a booth near the back. Her eyes landed on him. He was working his way through a plate piled high with what looked like a double cheeseburger and a mountain of fries. A half-empty milkshake glass sat beside him, condensation beading on its surface. There was weariness in his posture, a slump to his shoulders that suggested he wasn't simply enjoying a meal, but perhaps seeking a moment of solace.

"Hey, I didn't think you'd ever reach out to me after what happened last time," she said, sliding into the seat across from him.

"Please, sit," Bryson replied. He noticed she looked tired, dark circles under her eyes.

"I'm starving. The burgers look good here," said Sage as she picked up the menu.

"Their cheeseburgers are the best. The cheese fries and milkshakes are fire too," Bryson said. He took a sip from his drink.

"So, what's going on," said Sage, as she looked up from the menu.

"Thanks for coming," Bryson said, his voice low. He leaned forward, resting his elbows on the table. "I... I've been thinking a lot about what you said."

Sage nodded, her heart pounding in her chest. She wasn't sure what to expect. Apologies? More arguments? A flat-out refusal?

"About me not having the balls," Bryson continued, a flicker of a wry smile touching his lips. "You know, you have a real way of cuttin' through the bullshit, Sage."

"I just... I'm desperate," Sage said, her voice cracking slightly. "I don't know what else to do. It feels like everyone's just moving on, like Autumn never even existed."

Bryson's face softened. "I know. I feel it too. Every dang day. It's like... like there's this hole inside me, and nothing fits anymore." He paused, looking down at the formica tabletop. "And you're right. I can't just sit around and do nothing. I can't let whoever did this get away with it. Autumn... she deserves better. She deserves for us to fight for her."

Sage's eyes widened. "So... you're in? You want to help me?"

Bryson nodded, his expression serious.

"Yeah. I'm in. But," he held up a hand.

"On my terms. I'm not going back to that life, Sage. I'm not risking everythin' I've worked for. But I will do everything I can. Once we start, I'm prepared to do whatever it takes, within reason, to find this son of bitch."

"What does that mean, within reason?" Sage asked, a hint of suspicion in her voice.

"It means we gotta be smart about this, no confronting suspects alone, no half ass'n," Bryson said firmly. "I have a record. I can't afford to even look sideways at the feds. We gotta cover our tracks. We gotta use our connections. I will keep my eyes and ears open; you do the same. And I can help you figure out where to start."

Sage let out a breath she hadn't realized she'd been holding. It wasn't everything she wanted, but it was a start. A huge start. "Okay," she said, nodding. "Okay, I can work with that."

A waitress approached, a middle-aged woman with tired eyes and a warm smile.

"What can I get you hun?" she asked.

"I'll have a milkshake," Sage said, a sudden craving hitting her. "Chocolate."

As the waitress walked away, Bryson leaned in again. "So, tell me everything. Everything Autumn ever said, anything that seemed off, anything at all. We need to start putting the pieces together."

Sage began to talk, her words tumbling out in a rush. She told him about Autumn's fear, about the black eye, about the ripped shirt, about the secrets she kept. She told him about the feeling of being watched, the strange phone calls, the fleeting glimpses of a dark car parked down the street. She recounted every detail she could remember, no matter how insignificant it seemed.

"Autumn told me what happened," said Sage.

"What happened?" questioned Bryson.

"That you were wrongly accused of an agravated assault and ended up in prison. She told me it really affected y'all relationship."

Bryson sighed. "Yeah, I served two years at Blue Onion State Penitentiary for something I ain't do. Y'know wrong place at the wrong time. I was just defending myself."

Bryson adjusted his shirt.

"My brother went to prison for a few years too," Sage added.

"Where'd yo brother do his time?"

"Arrendale, I think that's the name," said Sage.

"I heard about that place. There's some tough dudes out there."

"It's messed up, isn't it?" Sage said softly. "My brother got out a year ago, and he's still trying to put his life back together."

"It's a long road," Bryson recounted, nodding slightly. "It's like... the world moved on while I was gone, and I had to catch up."

"It's a lot to deal with," Sage said.

"Yeah. But thinking about being wrongly accused still upsets me. I'd rather not talk about it anymore," Bryson responded.

"I understand," Sage said quietly, nodding slightly. "I'm sorry you went through that."

"It's cool," concluded Bryson.

The waitress returned with her drink, the chocolate milkshake thick and frosty. Bryson took a sip of his shake. "Okay," he said, setting down his glass. "That's a lot to work with. But it's a start. Let's start by figuring out who those secrets were about."

And as they sat there in the quiet corner of the Burger and Shake, surrounded by the comforting sounds of a small-town diner, they began to map out their plan.

Chapter 14- Sage, Bryson & Antoine

Sage navigated the maze of the narrow, unpaved roads leading to Antoine's trailer. The late afternoon sun cast long, distorted shadows, making the already desolate landscape seem even more eerie. Bryson sat beside her in the Honda Civic, as he admired the passing scenery.

"You sure about this, Sage?" Bryson finally asked.

"He's all I got," Sage replied. "And he owes me."

"Owes you what?" asked Bryson.

"His life," Sage said simply, her eyes straight ahead. "He messed up bad a few years back. I helped him out when no one else would...He'll do this for me."

The road twisted and turned, leading them further away from the main thoroughfares and deeper into a part of town that seemed forgotten by time. Weathered signs pointed to businesses long since closed, their paint peeling and fading in the relentless sun. Stray dogs roamed the cracked sidewalks, their ribs showing beneath their matted fur. They pulled up to a battered, faded blue trailer, its paint peeling like sunburnt skin. A rusty pickup truck sat on cinder blocks in the overgrown yard, and a couple of mangy-looking cats scattered under the porch. Empty beer cans littered the steps, glinting in the fading light. The place reeked of neglect and a certain kind of desperate freedom.

"Home sweet home," Sage announced, cutting the engine.

Bryson looked around, taking in the scene.

"He lives here?"

"Yeah. It's not much, but it's his. C'mon."

They walked up the rickety steps, and Sage knocked on the door. A moment later, the door creaked open, revealing a man with a wiry frame and a face etched with hard living. His arms were covered in a chaotic tapestry of tattoos, some faded, others fresh and vibrant. He had a scruffy beard, and his eyes, though bloodshot, held a spark of intelligence. He held a half-empty beer bottle in his hand, and the scent of marijuana clung to him.

"Sage," Antoine marveled, a hint of surprise in his voice. "Whatchu doin' all the way out here sissy?" He glanced at Bryson, his eyes narrowing slightly. "And who's this fucker?"

"This is Bryson," Sage said. "Autumn's brother."

Antoine's expression softened, a flicker of recognition in his eyes.

"Oh, What's good homie. I heard about what happened. Real sorry, man." He extended a hand to Bryson, who shook it firmly.

"Thanks," Bryson said.

"Can we come in, 'Toine?" Sage asked.

"Sure, sure," Antoine drawled, stepping aside. "Don't mind the mess. I ain't clean like y'all"

The inside of the trailer was cramped and cluttered. Half-finished drawings were scattered across a makeshift table, alongside tools, empty paint cans, and stacks of worn comic books. An old guitar leaned against the wall, its strings rusted, but its body bearing the marks of frequent use. Dirty dishes piled in the sink, clothes lay scattered on the floor, and the air was dense with the smell of beer and something vaguely medicinal. It wasn't just messy; it was a mess that spoke of a restless mind, of a spirit constantly creating and discarding, a life lived on the fringes, where rules were bent, and creativity flourished in the cracks.

Antoine gestured to a worn-out couch.

"Have a seat. I was just about to crack another one. You guys want anything?"

"No, thanks," Sage said. "I'm good brother, let's take care of business." Antoine raised an eyebrow, taking a long swig of his beer. "Business? What kind of business?"

"It's about Autumn," Sage said, her voice hardening. "About who killed her."

Antoine's eyes darkened. He set the beer bottle down on a cluttered table, the clink echoing in the small space. "The cops ain't found nobody?"

"They put the case on hold," Bryson interjected. "Said they hit a dead end."

Antoine cursed under his breath. "They never give a flyin' fuck about us."

"That's why we're doing this ourselves," Sage remarked. "I need your help, Antoine."

A part of Antoine recoiled at Sage's request. He'd tried to leave that life behind, to carve out a space for where he wasn't defined by his past mistakes. But another part of him, a darker, more restless part, felt a flicker of excitement. The prospect of a chase, of a mission, of fighting for something he believed in, ignited a spark within him. He knew this was dangerous, that it could drag him back into the very darkness he was trying to escape. But he also knew he couldn't refuse Sage, not after everything she'd done for him. He owed her, and maybe, just maybe, this was a chance to repay that debt.

Antoine looked at her, his expression softening. "Anything for my lil' sister. You know that. What do you need?"

"I need you to help us find whoever did this," Sage said. "I need your connections, your... your skills."

Antoine chuckled, a dry, humorless sound. "You mean you want me to get my hands dirty? You want this guy dead?" He took another swig of beer.

"I mean you know how the streets work," Sage replied. "You know people. You're not afraid of getting your hands dirty. And you're not afraid of going back to prison. Even though you won't be going back."

Antoine's pupils met hers, and for a second, there was something raw and vulnerable in his eyes.

"You always did know me too well, Sage-Marie. You always did. But I ain't going back to that hell hole," he looked at Bryson.

"And you? You in on this too, right?"

"I am," Bryson said firmly. "Autumn is my sister. I gotta handle my business."

Antoine nodded slowly. "Alright. I'm in. For Autumn, and for you, Sage. But let's get one thing straight. This ain't no game. This shit is dangerous. We talkin' 'bout a motherfucka who killed someone and got away with it. They ain't gon' be happy if we start poking around."

"We know," Sage said. "We're ready."

"And another thing," Antoine added.

"No backing down, no holding back. We go all the way, no matter what. You two with me on that?"

"All the way," Bryson repeated.

"Always," Sage said, her eyes meeting Antoine's.

Antoine grinned, a flash of his old, reckless self.

"Good. Now, let's get down to business. Tell me everything y'all know." He grabbed another beer from a cooler by the couch and cracked it open.

"And don't leave out a single fuckin' detail. I'm gon' need it all."

Antoine continued.

"What kinda fuckin' secrets are we talkin' here? Drug money? Some high-stakes card game gone sideways? Folks disappear and get murdered in that swamp for all sorts of reasons, and most of 'em ain't pretty," Antoine leaned back, eyeing a loose thread on his jeans. "Or was Autumn involved in somethin' she shouldn't have been? 'Cause if it's that kinda secret, then the swamp ain't the only thing tryin' to keep her quiet about it."

Bryson stepped forward.

"She was studying to be a nurse. She worked two jobs. She had a kid. She wasn't into that kinda life."

His face was a stone, unwavering.

"She was scared. Terrified, actually. Someone was following her, harassing her. And Sage found a journal. Autumn wrote about secrets that would ruin her if they came out."

Antoine's eyes, previously laced with casual cynicism, now held something new—a recognition of the seriousness in Bryson's tone. He knew the look of a man who was fighting to keep his past buried, a man who had more to lose than just words. He'd seen it in the mirror enough times.

"We need to know about those secrets," Sage interjected. "Who she was afraid of. Antoine, you know people. You hear things. Things that don't make it to the police blotter."

Antoine took another long swig from his beer. The hum of the refrigerator in the corner was the loudest sound. He ran a tattooed hand over his scruffy beard, his gaze distant, lost in the murky waters of his own memory. He'd seen the fear Autumn's type of secrets could breed. These weren't the simple, fleeting fears of a neighborhood spat. These were the kind that clung to you like kudzu, choking out everything else until all that was left was a bare, rattling bone.

"Alright," Antoine finally said, his voice flat. "Autumn... she was a smart girl. Too smart for some of the folks she ran with. Especially the kind of folks who don't like their business aired out. This ain't about petty grievances or a busted drug deal. This feels heavier. Like sinkin' your whole friggin' life in quicksand." He paused, looking directly at Bryson. "You look like a mothafucka who knows what it means to keep a secret."

Bryson didn't flinch. "I know enough to know that sometimes, secrets kill."

Antoine gave a short, humorless chuckle. "Truer words never been spoken, my guy. This swamp, it ain't just water and trees. It's got ears. And a memory. You gotta know how to listen to it, how to dig that shit where the ground is softest." He pointed a finger at Sage. "And that journal? That's our compass. What else did it say?"

Sage pulled a small, worn leather-bound notebook from her bag. "I haven't read much. It's... hard. But she mentioned someone. Not a name, not really. More like a description. She called him the collector. Said he had a way of finding things. And people. He never forgot a debt."

Antoine's eyes narrowed. "The collector? That ain't no name I know. But it sounds like a flippin' ghost story for grown-ups. The kind that gets whispered around campfires, you feel me? Nobody ever believes 'til it's too late. What kind of things was he collecting?"

"She ain't say," Sage admitted, flipping through the pages. "Just... things. And she drew a symbol." She turned the journal to a page with a sketch – a jagged, almost claw-like mark.

Bryson felt a jolt. An old incident near the swamp six months prior had the same symbol. The pieces were starting to connect, forming a monstrous, unsettling whole. This wasn't just a random act of violence. This was a pattern.

"This mark," Bryson said, pointing to the drawing. "The detectives found something similar at the swamp. Six months ago. A disturbance. Footprints... with claw-like impressions. And tire tracks from a truck."

Antoine rubbed his chin. "Well, ain't that somethin'. Six months, huh? The swamp keeps a long memory, especially when blood's been spilled. A collector... a mark... and a truck. This ain't no random punk-ass kids. This is organized. Someone with resources. Someone who knows how to make folks disappear without a trace. And the swamp? It's just their clean-up crew, their crematory."

A shiver ran down Sage's spine. The casual way Antoine spoke of lives being erased, the swamp as an accomplice, painted a chilling picture. She thought of Autumn, terrified, alone, hunted.

"So, what do we do?" Sage asked. "How do we find someone who doesn't want to be found?"

Antoine stood, walked to a dusty shelf, and pulled down a battered old map of the Everglades, spreading it out on the makeshift table. Its creases were worn, its edges frayed, a roadmap of hidden trails and forgotten inlets. "You gotta think like a tracker, sis. Like a predator. And like prey. You gotta understand the lay of the land. Not just the physical map, but the currents, the whispers, the unspoken rules of this town. Every debt, every secret, leaves a ripple. You just gotta know where to look for the waves."

He pointed to a cluster of handwritten notes scrawled in the margins of the map, notations about abandoned shacks, old logging trails, and places where the marsh swallowed everything whole. "There are eyes and ears in places the police ain't never gonna find. Folks who operate in the dark. They might know this *collector*. Or at least, they know who moves the *things* he collects. And they know who cleans up the messes."

Bryson leaned over the map, his mind racing. This was the wild, unpredictable heart of the Everglades, where rules were rewritten by survival and secrets were buried deeper than anybody. His father's words echoed in his mind: *The mind is a weapon. Use it wisely.*

"We gotta find out what Autumn was involved in," Bryson stated. "What was valuable enough to kill for?

And what kind of debt could be so unforgiving to kill her?"

Antoine nodded slowly. "Now you thinkin'. The swamp don't be playin' with folks who stir up old mud. But if you wanna find the truth, sometimes you gotta dive headfirst into the fuckin' muck." He looked from Bryson to Sage. "But we gotta understand. We go digging into these kinds of secrets, we ain't just looking for answers. We painting a fuckin' target on our backs."

He took one last gulp of his beer.

"The kind of folks who brand people and feed 'em to gators... they don't like witnesses. And they sure as hell don't like folks trying to unravel their work," said Antoine.

The trailer suddenly felt colder, despite the humid Florida air outside.

"We know the risks," Bryson said. The desire for justice, fierce and unshakeable, was a fire in his belly. It burned hotter than any fear of the law, hotter than any ghost from his past. He glanced at Sage, her face pale but determined, and then at Antoine, whose hardened eyes seemed to reflect the unforgiving depths of the swamp itself. They were standing on the precipice of something dangerous, something that could shatter their lives. But for Bryson, for the gaping wound Autumn's absence had left in their world, the risk was one they were now willing to take.

Chapter 15- Sage, Bryson & Antoine

The cramped interior of Antoine's beat-up Chevy Impala felt even smaller with three bodies packed inside. Clothes were piled into boxes on the backseat. The seats, cracked and worn, stuck to their skin in the Florida heat. Antoine, the driver, tapped a rhythm on the steering wheel, his eyes darting between the road and the rearview mirror. His tattoos seemed to writhe in the dim light of the dashboard; each one a story etched onto his skin. Sage sat beside him, she stared out the window, a mix of fast-food joints and pawn shops blurring into a monotonous backdrop. In the back, Bryson shifted uncomfortably, his long legs struggling for space. The tension in the car was palpable, a silent acknowledgment of the dangerous path they were venturing down.

"You sure about this, Antoine?" Sage asked, her voice barely above a whisper. "Going straight to her school? Isn't that a bit... obvious?"

"Obvious is good," Antoine replied, a wry grin spreading across his face. "Nobody expects obvious. Besides, where else we gonna start? We gotta start somewhere." He took a drag from a cigarette.

"And Trevor, he was her ex, right? He might know something. Or at least, he might have seen something," said Antoine.

"He dumped her two months ago," Bryson responded from the back. "Why would he know anything now?"

"People talk," Antoine answered, flicking ash out the window. "Especially when things go bad. He might've heard something through the grapevine. Or maybe... maybe she told him something before they broke up. Something she didn't tell anyone else."

***

They arrived at the university campus just as the last rays of sunlight were fading. The buildings, usually bustling with students, were now quiet and deserted, their windows like dark, unblinking eyes. Antoine parked in a dimly lit corner of the lot, the Impala's engine sputtering to a halt.

"Alright," Antoine said, turning to face them. "Here's the plan. We stick together. We ask Trevor some questions. We don't threaten him, unless we absolutely have to. And we keep our fucking mouths shut about our own investigation. Got it?"

Bryson and Sage nodded in agreement. They got out of the car, the quietness of the campus pressing in around them. They found the building where Trevor supposedly hung out, a small, nondescript structure tucked away behind the main library. Inside, the lights hummed, casting a sterile glow on the empty hallways.

"His lab is down here," Sage said, pointing to a door at the end of the corridor. They approached cautiously, their footsteps echoing in the stillness. Antoine knocked, the sound sharp and insistent.

A moment later, the door opened, revealing a young man with tousled blond hair. He looked surprised to see them.

"Yeah?" he asked, hesitantly.

"Yo name Trevor, kid?" Antoine asked, stepping forward. "We need to talk to you. It's about Autumn."

Trevor took a step back. "Hey Sage?"

"Hey Trevor," Sage said quickly.

"How'd y'all know I was gonna be here?"

"Autumn, she told me this was ya'lls hangout spot after school. That you're the lab monitor. You help students with all the lab equipment," said Sage. "We just want to ask you a few questions."

"About what?" Trevor questioned, his voice laced with suspicion.

"About what happened to her," Bryson said. "About who might have wanted to hurt her."

Trevor's face blanched. "I... I don't know anything. We broke up, remember, Sage? I haven't seen her in weeks."

"We know y'all broke up, idiot," Antoine gibed, stepping closer. "But we also know you cared about her. And we think you might know something. Something that could help us find out who did this. Unless...unless you the one that did it."

Trevor hesitated, his eyes shifting between the three of them. He looked like he wanted to shut the door in their faces, but something in their expressions, perhaps the sheer intensity of their determination, made him reconsider.

"Okay," he said finally, stepping aside. "Come in."

The lab was small and cluttered, filled with beakers, test tubes, and the faint smell of chemicals. Trevor gestured to a couple of stools, and they sat down.

"So," Trevor began, his voice still hesitant. "What do you want to know?"

"Did she ever mention anyone bothering her?" Sage asked. "Anyone following her? Anyone threatening her?"

Trevor shook his head. "Not to me. We hadn't been talking much before... before all of this. But when we were together, she never said anything about being scared or anything."

"What about secrets?" Bryson asked. "Did she ever mention any secrets? Things she was keeping from people?"

Trevor paused. "She was... private. She ain't share a lot. But secrets? I dunno. Maybe. Everyone has secrets, right?"

Antoine leaned forward, his eyes narrowing.

"Okay, smartass. Did she ever mention anyone... unusual? Anyone who seemed out of place? Anyone you ain't recognize?"

Trevor thought briefly, then shook his head.

"Nah. Not really. But... but there was this one time. A few weeks before we broke up. I saw her getting into a car. A dark sedan with a missing hubcap. I ain't recognize the driver. And she seemed... nervous. Like she didn't want me to see her."

"A dark sedan?" Sage repeated, her voice rising slightly. "Did you get a look at the car? What kind was it?"

"I don't know," Trevor said, shrugging. "Just... dark. Maybe black? It wasn't anything fancy. Just a regular car. Old, maybe. A bit beat up."

"And the driver?" Bryson asked. "What did he look like?"

"I didn't get a good look," Trevor said. "It was dark. And he was wearing a hat. But... he was big. Tall. Broad shoulders."

"Did she say who he was?" Sage asked.

"No," Trevor said. "She just... she told me she had to go. And then she got in the car and they drove off. I tried to ask her about it later, but she just brushed it off. Said it was nothing."

"And where the heck did you see this car before?" Antoine asked.

"I saw it parked down the street from her apartment a few times. I thought it was weird, but I didn't think much of it."

"Where were you the night she died, Trevor?" Sage asked, her voice suddenly sharp.

Trevor's eyes were alert.

"What? Why would you ask me that? I was... I was here. In the lab. I was here all night. You can ask Professor Davies and all the students. They saw me."

Antoine exchanged a glance with Sage and Bryson. It was clear that Trevor was telling the truth. He seemed genuinely surprised and upset by their questions, not like someone who was trying to hide something.

"Alright, Trevor," Antoine said, his voice softening slightly. "We believe you. We just… we had to ask. We gon' find out who did this."

"I understand," Trevor said, his voice subdued. "I want to know too. Autumn… she didn't deserve this."

They talked for a little longer, asking Trevor about anything else he could remember, any other details that might be helpful. He didn't have much more to offer, but they took everything he said, every small detail, and filed it away in their minds.

"Trevor," Sage said finally, as they were getting ready to leave. "We need you to do something for us. We need you to keep this conversation between us. Don't tell anyone we were here. Don't tell anyone what we asked you. Can you do that?"

Trevor nodded slowly. "Yeah. Yeah, I can do that. I just… I hope you find out who did this."

"We will," Bryson said, his voice firm. "We promise you that."

They had a small lead, a dark sedan with a missing hubcap, and a tall driver. It wasn't much, but it was a start. It was something to hold on to.

"So," Sage said, as they piled back into the Impala. "What do we do now?"

"Easy, we don't stop till we find that car," Antoine said.

Chapter 16- Sage, Bryson & Antoine

"Man, did you see the way his eyes bugged out?" Antoine chuckled, a low rumble in his chest. "Like we were about to put him in a body bag."

Sage snorted, a small smile tugging at the corner of her mouth. "He looked like he was about to faint. I almost felt sorry for him."

"Almost?" Bryson chimed in from the back, stretching his arms. "C'mon, Sage, you were practically glowing with the interrogation vibes. I thought you were gonna make him confess to everything from stealing lunch money to the murder of Henry & Harriette Moore."

"Hey, I was just trying to get some answers," Sage retorted, though a hint of amusement colored her tone. "Besides, you were practically staring holes through him. Like you could see right into his soul."

"Someone had to keep him honest," Bryson stated, but there was a lightness in his voice, a camaraderie that hadn't been there before. The shared experience, the shared mission, was slowly knitting them together.

"Alright, enough ribbin'," Antoine advised, his eyes scanning the road. "Let's focus. Dark sedan, missing hubcap. That's what we looking for."

Hours blurred into a fruitless hunt through dimly lit streets and silent neighborhoods. No dark sedan with a missing hubcap appeared, only frustration. The city seemed to stretch on endlessly, a labyrinth of asphalt and concrete.

"It's like looking for a needle in a haystack," Sage sighed, rubbing her tired eyes. "Maybe Trevor was wrong. Maybe he imagined the whole thing."

"Or maybe," Bryson said, his voice thoughtful, "He just hiding shit. People remember things differently when they scared."

"Or maybe the guy fixed the hubcap," Antoine added. "Wouldn't be the first time."

The hours blurred into a rhythm of driving, scanning, and discussing. But amidst the frustration, they found themselves talking about other things too.

Bryson traced the outline of a faded tattoo on his forearm, a crude depiction of a coiled snake.

"This? Got this inside. Guy named Needles did it with a sewing pin and ink from a pen. Hurt like hell, but... it was a mark. A reminder." He paused as he looked out the window. The rain pattered against the glass; each drop a tiny drumbeat.

"Inside, you learn to make marks. On yo'self, on others. Just to prove you're still there. Still something." He rubbed the tattoo, the gesture almost tender. "But the marks you really carry... they're the ones you can't see. The ones that dig under your skin and stay there."

"That's cool, Bryson. I got a few tattoos myself," said Sage. She perched on the edge of her seat, fiddled with a stray thread on her worn denim jacket. The jacket was covered in patches, each one a souvenir from a different place, a different memory. "I want to build worlds," she said, her voice barely above a whisper. She gestured vaguely with her hand, her fingers tracing patterns in the air. "Not like... real worlds, but... stories. Places where people can go and... feel. Feel things they don't get to feel in their own lives. Like... like flying, or fighting dragons, or falling in love with someone who actually sees them, you know?" She bit her lip, a flicker of vulnerability in her eyes.

"I have this notebook, filled with scraps of ideas, half-formed characters, places that exist only in my head. But... sometimes, it feels like they're trapped in there. Like I can't find the words to set them free." She pulled a worn leather-bound notebook from her bag, its edges frayed, its pages dog-eared. The cover was covered in doodles, sketches of faces and places, a testament to her restless imagination.

"I guess I gotta join this story sharing bullshit, huh?" said Antoine. The lines around his eyes deepened as he spoke, etching themselves into his skin. "I gotta brother on my father's side of the family. Sage met him a few times," he said, his voice rough, like gravel grinding against stone. "We were thick as thieves. Always getting into trouble. Stupid shit, mostly. But... then I made a mistake." He clenched his jaw, the muscle twitching in his cheek. "A bad one. And... he paid for it. Not me. Him. I lost him. Lost everything. And now...," Antoine was lost in a memory only he could see. He reached up and touched a small, silver chain around his neck, a chain that glinted in the dim light. "This was his," he said softly. "Always with me. Always reminding me."

"Hey, look!" Sage suddenly sputtered, pointing to a car parked on the side of the road. "Missing hubcap!"

They all leaned forward, their hopes rising. But as they got closer, they saw that the car was white, not dark.

"Horse shit!" Antoine huffed, slapping the steering wheel. "We've been driving for hours. Nothing."

"Let's try one more spot," urged Bryson, his voice determined. "Back near the school. Maybe we'll get lucky."

***

They drove back to the university area, parking in a lot next to a dumpster. The car was positioned so they had a clear view of the school's main entrance. The engine idled, the hum a low, constant drone.

"We'll just wait here for a bit," Antoine said, lighting another cigarette. "See if anything turns up."

Time stretched on, slowly and agonizing. The city noises faded into a distant hum, replaced by the quiet rustle of leaves and the occasional passing car. The two men eventually drifted off to sleep, their heads lolling against the seats. But Sage stayed awake, her eyes fixed on the school, her mind racing with possibilities.

Then, she saw it. A dark sedan, sleek and menacing, pulled up to the curb near the school's entrance. Her heart leaped into her throat. The car had hubcaps, yes, but she couldn't see the other side. A tall man stepped out, his features obscured by the darkness. He moved with quiet confidence, a sense of purpose that sent electrical impulses down Sage's spine.

"Guys," she whispered, shaking Bryson's shoulder. "Guys, wake up!"

Bryson stirred, his eyes blinking open. "What? What's up?"

"A car," Sage blurted. "A dark sedan. It just pulled up."

Antoine woke up to the ruckus. "Where?"

Sage pointed to the car.

"Over there. By the school."

They all stared, their senses on high alert. Antoine cut the engine and turned off the lights, plunging the car into darkness.

"See the hubcaps?" Bryson whispered.

"I can't see the other side," Sage replied. "But that guy... he's tall. Like Trevor said."

"Let's see where he goes," Antoine added, his hand hovering over the ignition.

The tall man disappeared into the school, leaving the dark sedan idling at the curb. They waited, their breaths held, their muscles tense. Then, the man reappeared, walking back to the car with the same quiet confidence. He got in, and the sedan pulled away from the curb.

"Y'all ready?" Antoine's voice was low, intense. "Let's follow him."

The car engine roared to life, a rumble vibrating through the vehicle. He flicked the headlights on, then immediately switched them off. Slowly, carefully, they pulled out of the parking lot, all eyes fixed on the dark sedan as it disappeared into the night. The chase had begun.

Chapter 17- Sage, Bryson & Antoine

The Impala glided through the night. Antoine drove with a focused intensity, his hands gripping the steering wheel, knuckles white. The headlights remained off, plunging them into near-total darkness, except for the sliver of moonlight filtering through the canopy of Spanish moss-draped oaks that lined the road.

"He's turning," Sage whispered. Her eyes were glued to the dark sedan ahead. The sedan signaled abruptly, taking a sharp right onto a narrow, pothole-riddled road. Antoine reacted instantly, yanking the wheel and following.

"That's it," Sage breathed, her voice filled with a mix of excitement and dread. "That's the car. The one Trevor described. The one with the missing hubcap."

She pointed to the rear wheel of the car. In the dim light, the absence was unmistakable, a dark void where metal should have been.

Bryson leaned forward from the back seat. "So, it wasn't just Trevor's imagination. There really is a car. And a tall guy."

The car continued down the dilapidated road. Houses thinned out, replaced by stretches of overgrown fields and patches of dense, impenetrable woods. The sense of isolation grew.

Then, the car slowed, its brake lights flashing red in the night. It turned again, this time, onto a long, gravel driveway that disappeared into the dark. As they got closer, they saw the glow of distant lights, the outline of a large, boxy structure against the night sky. A warehouse.

"He's going in there," Bryson observed.

Antoine slowed the Impala, bringing it to a halt a short distance from the entrance. A tall, chain-link fence stretched across the opening, a heavy gate barring the way. Floodlights mounted on the warehouse illuminated the gate and the surrounding area.

"Fuck! We can't follow him in there," Antoine cursed, his voice filled with frustration. "There's a gate."

"Dang it," Sage exploded, slamming a fist against the dashboard. "We were so close."

"Not close enough," Bryson said, his eyes scanning the area. "There's a side road just up ahead. We can park there, out of sight."

Antoine nodded, pulling his car forward and turning onto the side road. They found a spot hidden behind a thicket of palmetto bushes, the car now completely obscured from view. He killed the engine.

"Cool, we good," Bryson assured. "What now?"

"We wait," Antoine replied, his voice calm but resolute. "We wait and see what he does."

The only sounds were the rustling of leaves and the occasional chirp of crickets.

"Why the school?" Sage suddenly asked, breaking the silence. "Why would he go there in the middle of the night? It doesn't make any sense."

"Maybe he works there," Bryson offered. "Janitor, security guard, something like that."

"At this hour?" Sage countered. "And why was he so secretive? Why didn't he just park in the school lot?"

"Maybe he was doing something he didn't want anyone to see, sis. He's probably a killer. Trust me, I know," said Antoine, as he gripped his .45 from beneath the seat.

"Like what?" Sage pressed. "What could he be doing at a school in the middle of the night?"

"Maybe he's hiding something," Bryson suggested. "Maybe he's stashing something there. Or picking something up."

"Drugs?" Sage asked.

"Could be," Bryson replied. "Or weapons. Or something else entirely."

"Or maybe," Antoine said, a dark edge creeping into his voice. "Maybe that fuck boy is planning something. Something bad."

The image of Autumn, discarded in the swamp, flashed through Sage's mind.

"We need to know," Sage said. "We need to know what he's doing in that warehouse. And why he was at the school."

"Just chill, we will," Bryson avowed, his eyes glinting in the moonlight. "But we need to be smart about this. We can't just rush in there. We need a plan."

They fell silent again, each lost in their own thoughts. The questions swirled around them, unanswered, unsettling. Who was this man? What was he hiding? And what did he have to do with Autumn's death? The answers were out there, somewhere, hidden, waiting to be uncovered.

The night deepened. They waited, their eyes fixed on the gate, their hearts pounding with a mixture of fear and anticipation. They were in too deep to turn back now.

Chapter 18- Bugsy & The Crew

The warehouse wasn't the place you stumbled upon
by accident. Tucked away deep in the industrial outskirts
of town, past the rusting train tracks and the overgrown
lots, it stood like a forgotten relic of a bygone era. Inside,
it reeked stale beer, cheap cigars, and something else,
something akin to desperation.

Bugsy sat at the head of a rickety table. His eyes,
small and dark like chips of obsidian, scanned the room,
taking in every detail, every subtle shift in the
atmosphere. He tapped a cigarette against the chipped
ashtray, the rhythmic sound a nervous counterpoint to
the oppressive quietness.

Around him, his crew shifted uneasily. There was
Earl, the tall guy, his lanky frame hunched over. Earl was
the muscle, the driver, the one who did the dirty work
without asking too many questions. Then there was

Weasel, a wiry, twitchy man with eyes that moved around like trapped mice. Weasel was the informant, the one who knew things. And finally, there was Junior, young and eager, but with a simmering violence that made Bugsy uneasy.

"We got a problem," Bugsy began, his words throaty. "A real problem."

A nervous energy rippled through the room. They all knew what that meant. Problems meant trouble, and trouble meant the man upstairs wasn't happy. And when the man upstairs wasn't happy, things got messy.

"He called," Bugsy continued, his gaze sweeping over his crew. "Said we tied up one loose end, but another one's still dangling. The kid... the dead girl's ex-boyfriend. Turns out, he knows more than we thought."

Earl shifted in his seat. He remembered Trevor. A skinny, nervous kid who'd always seemed to be on edge. He'd seen him at the school, his eyes wide and wary, as if he knew he was being watched.

"So, what are we supposed to do?" Weasel's high-pitched whine interjected. "We've looked everywhere for the kid".

"Find him," Bugsy confirmed.

"Before he finds someone else to talk to. Before he spills what he knows."

"But he gone," Junior kissed his teeth, his voice tinged with impatience. "He quit his job. Took off like a ghost."

"Ghosts can be found," Bugsy replied, a cruel glister in his eyes. "They leave traces. Whispers in the wind. And we're gonna find those whispers."

He leaned forward, his brows powerful.

"We been watchin' that school, like you said. Every day. It's like he just disappeared. But that don't happen, right? People don't just vanish. They go somewhere. They talk to someone."

Earl thought back to his visit to the school. He was there earlier during the day asking random college kids if they knew of a blond kid that looked like the rapper, Eminem. The students looked at him and laughed. *"Trevor has blond hair, but he looks nothing like Eminem,"* cackled a student.

During the interaction Earl had lost his necklace. So, he went back during the night hoping to find it. He remembered the quiet, the eerie stillness of the empty hallways. Luckily, he found his chain, shimmering under a light post just outside the building, but something else had caught his attention. A dark Impala, parked across the street, its lights off.

"Bugsy," Earl began. "I saw somethin' tonight. When I went back to the school."

"What?" Bugsy asked, his eyes narrowing.

"A car. An Impala. Parked across the street. Lights off."

Bugsy's eyes sharpened. "Five-O?"

"Didn't think so. It was just sittin' there. Then, when I started to leave, it took off."

"Could've been anyone," Weasel said dismissively.

"Maybe," Earl replied, but something in his gut told him it was more than that. Something about the way the car had been positioned.

"That's it?" Bugsy said.

Earl recounted the details, the quiet street, the dark car, the feeling of being watched. Bugsy listened intently, his face unreadable.

"Could be nothin'," he said finally. "But we can't take no chances. Weasel, I want you to dig. Find out everything you can about that kid. Where he lived, who he talked to, where he might have gone."

Weasel nodded, his eyes dancing nervously. "Sure thing, Bugsy."

"Junior," Bugsy continued, turning to the younger man. "I want you to keep an eye on the school. Watch for anything unusual. Any strangers, any suspicious cars."

Junior grinned, a flash of something dangerous in his eyes. "Got it, Bugsy."

"And Earl," Bugsy said. "I want you to retrace your steps. Go back to the school tonight. See if you see that Impala again. But be careful. We don't know who's in it, or what they want."

Earl nodded, an unease settled in his stomach. He didn't like the idea of going back to the school, not after what he'd seen. But he knew he had no choice. Bugsy's orders were not to be disobeyed.

Later that night, Earl found himself back at the school. He parked his car a block away and walked the rest of the way, his senses heightened.

The school looked different at night. The familiar buildings seemed larger, more imposing, shrouded in shadows. The parking lot was empty. Earl walked slowly as he scanned the darkness, searching for any sign of the Impala.

Then he saw it. The dark Impala driving by.

Earl froze, his hand instinctively going to the pocket where he kept his knife. He felt a surge of fear, but also a gush of adrenaline. He had to know who was in that car, what they wanted.

He started to walk towards the Impala, his footsteps slow and deliberate. He kept to the shadows, using the trees and the buildings for cover. He could feel his heart pounding in his chest.

As he got closer, he could see that there were figures inside the car. He couldn't make out their faces, but he could see their silhouettes, dark and indistinct. He stopped, his hand tightening on his knife.

Suddenly, the Impala roared to life. The headlights flashed on, blindingly bright, and the car lurched forward. Earl jumped back, narrowly avoiding being hit. The Impala sped past him.

Earl stooped there, catching his breath, his heart still racing, body shaking. He watched as the Impala's taillights faded into the distance, leaving him alone in the quiet street.

Chapter 19- Sage, Bryson & Antoine

The tires screamed against the asphalt as Antoine swerved. Earl, a spectral figure in the dim light, had materialized like a bad portent, and only Antoine's reflexes had saved him from becoming a hood ornament. Sage, gripped the dashboard, knuckles white as bone. Bryson in the back, just grunted, a sound that spoke volumes of his simmering rage. The rain hammered down, each drop a tiny explosion against the roof. The neon glow of a distant gas station sign painted the interior in sickly hues of pink and green.

"Holy shit!" Antoine yelled, hands still clenched around the steering wheel. "Almost killed that fool."

He glanced in the rearview, but Earl was gone, swallowed by the darkness. "Who was that?"

"Not sure but it looked like a tall guy," Bryson said from the back.

Sage shuddered. "He looked... lost. Like he didn't even see us."

"He saw us," Antoine said, his eyes fixed on the rearview mirror. "He just didn't expect us. Nobody expects us."

***

They drove for a while. Bryson kept glancing over his shoulder, half-expecting to see headlights following them, but the road remained empty. The tension in the car didn't evanesce; it merely mutated into reticence. Finally, they pulled off the highway and onto a narrow dirt road that led deeper into the pines. Antoine's trailer home sat nestled among the trees.

They made their way up the trailer steps and into his house after parking.

"Hmm," Antoine grumbled. "We need a plan. And we need it now." He pulled a bottle of whiskey from a cupboard and took a long swig. "First thing first, Sage, you ain't goin' back to your place. Not tonight. They know where you live."

Sage shook her head; her eyes filled with defiance. "I can't just—I have all my stuff there."

"You can and you will. Your stuff don't mean shit if you're dead," Antoine interrupted, slamming the bottle on the table. "This ain't a request. It's an order. They see you, they see us. You're stayin' here."

Bryson nodded in agreement. "He's right, Sage. It's too risky."

Sage looked from one to the other, her initial resistance slowly fading. She knew they were right. She was a liability, and she didn't want to drag them down. But more than that, she was scared. Scared of being alone, petrified of what might happen if she went home by herself.

"Okay," she said finally. "Okay, I'll stay."

Antoine grunted, a flicker of approval in his eyes. He went to a battered metal box in the corner and pulled out a gun, well-worn .38. He handed it to Bryson. "You know how to use this, right?"

Bryson took the gun, its weight familiar in his hand. He ran a thumb over the cold steel. "Yeah," he said. "Yeah, I know."

"Good," Antoine replied. "Because you gonna need it," He looked at Bryson, his eyes hard and unwavering.

Bryson met his gaze. "Whatever it takes. I failed her before. I won't fail her again."

The two men stood there, the gun a silent testament to their shared purpose, the room filled with an unspoken vow. They were bound together by grief and rage, and they would not rest until justice was served. Sage watched them, a mixture of trepidation and determination swirling within her. She knew this was dangerous, that they were playing a game with high stakes, but she also knew there was no turning back. They were in this together, and they would see it through to the end.

"Autumn would've hated this," Sage said suddenly. "All the violence, the guns... she just wanted peace. She wanted everyone to be okay."

Antoine's face mellowed.

"I know, sis," he consoled. "But sometimes, you gotta fight for peace. Sometimes, you gotta get your hands dirty to make things right."

Bryson nodded. "My sister wouldn't want us to just... roll over. She'd want us to fight. To find the truth."

Sage looked at them, her eyes filled with tears. "Then let's fight for her," she said, her voice gaining strength. "Let's find the truth. And let's make sure... let's make sure they never hurt anyone again."

Chapter 20- Bugsy & The Crew

Bugsy traced the rim of his beer bottle with his nicotine-stained finger, the lager doing little to quench the fire burning in his gut. The lights of the Dew Drop Inn cast a sickly pallor on the faces of his crew.

"So," Bugsy said. "We clear on the play?"

Weasel nodded sharply.

"The dead girl's place. Check for anything that links to that kid, or whoever was driving that Impala. If they tried to clip Earl, they ain't playing nice."

Bugsy looked away. "Exactly why we gotta move smart. In and out. No noise, no mess. Understand?"

Weasel fidgeted in his seat, the vinyl squeaking beneath him. "What if they're still there? Watching?"

"Then we dance," Bugsy said. "But we dance to our own tune. Remember, we ain't looking to kill anyone, we looking for answers."

Junior rubbed his hands together. "And if we find somethin'? Somethin' that points to who's behind this?"

Bugsy's gaze hardened. "Then we bring it back. To me. And then... then we decide what song we're gonna play." He took a long pull from his beer, the bitterness coating his tongue.

They left the bar in a tight knot. Earl drove. Bugsy sat shotgun. The other two in the backseat.

Autumn's apartment building was a tired brick structure, tucked away on a side street. Earl parked a few blocks away, and they slipped out of the car, making their way to the apartment building.

"Third floor, back right," Bugsy questioned, checking the address scribbled on a crumpled piece of paper. "Let's do this."

The stairs creaked beneath their weight, each sound amplified in the stillness of the building. The air smelled of cooking oil and something vaguely floral, a cloying sweetness that made Bugsy's nose twitch. They reached the third floor, the hallway stretching out before them, a dim tunnel of closed doors.

"Remember," Bugsy whispered, "We just visiting."

He tested the doorknob of Autumn's apartment.

"Locked," he whispered. Junior produced a slim set of tools from his pocket, working with a practiced ease that spoke of years spent on the wrong side of the law. A soft click, and the door swung inward.

The apartment was small, but tidy, a testament to Sage and Autumn's organized nature. A few framed photos sat on a bookshelf, capturing moments of laughter and friendship. A half-finished book lay open on the coffee table, its pages slightly yellowed. The air smelled faintly of vanilla and something else, something personal, something that made Bugsy's chest tighten.

"Split up," Bugsy commanded. "Junior, bedrooms. Weasel, living room. Earl, you're the lookout, stay at the front door. I'll take the kitchen and any papers we find."

They moved through the apartment with quiet efficiency, their movements practiced and purposeful. Junior sifted through drawers, his touch light but thorough. Weasel examined every corner of the living room, missing nothing. Bugsy went through the kitchen cabinets, finding little more than mismatched dishes and a few dusty spice jars.

"Anything?" Bugsy called out.

"Nothing here but clothes and a bunch of girly stuff," Junior announced from the bedroom. "And a whole lot of yellow."

"Yellow?" Bugsy puzzled.

"Yeah, everything's yellow. Walls, curtains, even some of the damn clothes. Weird."

Bugsy started going through the drawers again, this time with more intent. He was not looking just at the clothing, but underneath, behind, and within. He found a journal tucked under a stack of sweaters. The cover was worn; the pages filled with Autumn's neat, looping handwriting. He flipped through it, his eyes scanning the words, searching for a clue, a hint, anything.

"What's that?" Weasel asked, nodding toward the journal.

"The dead girl's diary," Bugsy said. "Let's see what secrets she was keeping."

He started to read aloud. The entries were mostly mundane, filled with details of daily life, classes, friends, hopes, and dreams. But then, he found an entry that made him pause.

I feel like they're gonna try to kill me. I know too much for them to let me live. Every time I see them I feel like I'm about to die. I don't know what to do or who to tell. I can't even tell, Sage.

Bugsy flipped through more pages, finding other similar entries, each one more unsettling than the last. Autumn's fear had been growing, her anxiety escalating. She had felt trapped, hunted.

I can't tell anyone. They wouldn't believe me. They'd think I'm paranoid. Then I'd end up dead. But I know what I know. I know what I feel. I'm not safe.

"She knew," Bugsy acknowledged. "She knew something was coming."

Bugsy closed the journal. "Who the fuck is Sage?"

Weasel then stepped out of Autumn's room and walked to the other door in the hallway. He opened it and stepped inside. "This room is different," he called out to Bugsy. "More... lived in, but not in the same way. Look at this." He held up a framed photo of Sage with a different group of friends, clearly from a different stage in her life. "This isn't Autumn's stuff."

Bugsy made his way to the room. He stepped inside and took in the surroundings. Unlike Autumn's bright, yellow-themed room, this one had a darker, more bohemian feel. Tapestries hung on the walls, covering some of the peeling paint. Bookshelves overflowed with paperbacks, and a small desk was cluttered with notebooks and art supplies. The bed was unmade, with a patchwork quilt thrown haphazardly over it. It was clear this was someone else's space, someone with a different personality and style.

"This must be the other girl's room," Bugsy said, his eyes scanning the space. "Sage."

Junior joined them, peering into the room. "Explains why there's two bedrooms. Makes sense." He shrugged. "So? What's that tell us?"

"It tells us we need to check here too," Bugsy said, moving further into the room. He started opening drawers, his movements quick and efficient. He found more photos, some of Sage alone, some with her brother, and some with Autumn. He found a box of letters, tied together with a ribbon. He didn't bother reading them. He was looking for something more concrete, something that would lead them to Trevor or the Impala driver.

He continued to search, and in the back of the closet, behind a box of old shoes, he found a small, locked metal box. He looked at Junior who simply nodded his head. With a quick flick of his wrist, the lock sprung open. Inside, they found a stack of photos, a burner phone, and a small, intricately folded piece of paper.

The photos were candid shots of a man, his face obscured by distance. The burner phone was wiped clean, its memory empty. But the folded paper, when unfolded, revealed a handwritten note, scrawled in a hurried hand.

"Meet at the old mill, midnight. Don't be late. And don't bring anyone."

"Old mill?" Junior said. "Where the hell is that?"

"Out past the county line," Bugsy said, his eyes scanning the note. "Been abandoned for years. Perfect place for a meet... or a setup."

Junior's voice was hard. "When was this written?"

Bugsy looked at the note again, his eyes tracing the date at the top. "Three days before... before she died."

A stillness fell over the room, followed by the soft ticking of a clock on the bedside table. They stood there, the journal, the photos, the phone, and the note spread out before them, each item a piece of the puzzle.

Chapter 21- Sage, Bryson & Antoine

The Florida sun heated the aluminum roof, turning the inside into a sweltering oven. A single, rattling window unit coughed out lukewarm air, barely stirring the dust bunnies dancing in the morning light. Sunlight bled through the cheap blinds, striping the linoleum floor like prison bars. Antoine was cleaning his shotgun. Bryson sat at the chipped table, nursing a lukewarm cup of instant coffee, his eyes filled with worry. Sage shifted uncomfortably on the worn-out sofa, her face drawn.

"Look, y'all, "she began, "I gotta... I gotta run to the store."

Antoine's head snapped up, his dark eyes narrowing. "Store? What for? We got enough grits and beans to last a week."

"It's... it's personal stuff. Lady things," Sage mumbled, fiddling with the frayed hem of her cutoff shorts. "Just a quick run to the Piggly Wiggly, grab a few things, and I'll be right back. In and out, quick as a jackrabbit."

Antoine studied her, his brow furrowed. "You sure? We said stay put, Sagey. Things ain't exactly sunshine and roses out there."

"I know, I know," she said, her voice a tad too high. "It's daytime," she insisted, trying to sound more confident than she felt. "Ain't nobody gonna mess with me in broad daylight. Besides–," she added with a weak smile, "A girl's gotta keep herself together."

"Bet, but you be quick, sis. No detours, no sightseeing. Ya hear?"

"Yeah, yeah, I got it," Sage said, grabbing her purse. "Just a few things. In and out."

As she slipped out the door, Bryson and Antoine exchanged a worried glance. "She's lyin'," Bryson urged. "I can smell it on her like cheap perfume."

"She's always been a stubborn little brat," Antoine shrugged, but his eyes held a hint of malaise. "But she wouldn't be stupid enough to go back there."

Sage climbed into her Honda Civic. Her destination was her apartment, the one place they'd all agreed she should stay away from. But she needed clothes, a few personal items, something that felt like her. Nobody would be watching at this hour. She drove with a jitteriness, the sun bouncing off the cracked windshield, the radio playing a scratchy gospel tune.

She pulled up to her apartment building, parking haphazardly at the curb, the car still running. Sage knew she shouldn't be here. Antoine had been clear: *Stay away. They know where you live.* She parked, killed the engine, sat for a moment scanning the parking lot. A few cars she recognized. Mrs. Chen's Toyota. The maintenance guy's truck. Nothing unusual. She stepped out of the car; the pavement felt hard beneath her feet. She told herself it would be quick. Just grab a few things and go. The street was deserted, the morning quiet. The distant drone of lawnmowers filled the air. She felt watched, as if unseen eyes were tracking her every move. She glanced around, saw nothing, and hurried towards the building's entrance. The feeling persisted, a nagging discomfort that refused to fade. She pushed the feeling down, telling herself it was just her nerves, the lingering fear from the previous night's encounter.

The elevator doors slid open with a soft hiss, and she stepped inside, pressing the button for her floor. As the elevator ascended, she felt a strange sense of detachment, as if she were watching herself from afar, a character in a movie she desperately wanted to escape.

The elevator doors opened, and Sage stepped out into the hallway. She noticed the faint hum of the building's ventilation system. She moved quickly, her footsteps muffled by the carpet, her eyes fixed on her apartment door. As she reached it, she fumbled with her keys, her hands shaking slightly. Just as she was about to unlock the door, two figures emerged, their movements swift and silent.

"Well, well, look what we got here," a voice drawled, thick with menace.

Sage froze, her heart hammering against her ribs. Junior, his face a mask of cold indifference, and Weasel with his twitchy, rat-like energy, stood blocking her path. Before she could react, Weasel moved, his hand grabbing her arm in a vice-like grip. She tried to pull away, to scream, but Junior was faster. His hand flashed out, a brutal slap that sent her head reeling. A searing pain exploded in her lip, and the metallic taste of blood filled her mouth. She stumbled back, her vision blurring, the hallway tilting around her.

"You ain't goin' nowhere, sweetheart," Junior growled.

They dragged her into the apartment, the familiar space suddenly feeling alien and threatening. They shoved her onto the couch, their faces inches from hers, their eyes boring into her.

"What do you know?" Weasel demanded, his voice sharp and insistent. "About Trevor. You know him. Autumn's ex. Where is he?""

Sage remained silent, her eyes blazing with defiance despite the fear that clawed at her insides. Junior's fist caught her in the stomach. The air left her lungs in a rush. She doubled over, would have collapsed if he wasn't holding her up by her hair. They kept asking, their questions turning into threats, then blows. Each punch landed like a hammer, blurring her vision, stealing her breath. They taunted her, saying they'd do to her what they did to Autumn, but she refused to break. She'd sooner die than give them anything.

Junior's face hovered close, his breath hot. "We ain't playing games, girlie. You keep quiet or you gon' end up like your roommate."

Rage flared through the pain. Sage spat blood in his face. His expression didn't change. He wiped the blood away slowly, deliberately. Then he hit her again. And again. The world became a blur of impact and pain. She tasted more blood, felt her eye swelling shut, heard a ringing in her ears that wouldn't stop.

She glared at Junior through swollen eyes. She knew this creep. Arlo's boy. She didn't know Weasel at all. But him? She knew him, her ex-boyfriend's friend. She saw the flicker of recognition in his eyes, a question forming, but he shook his head as if to dismiss it.

"You think you scare me?" she whispered, her voice hoarse but strong. "You think you can get away with this?"

"Best we finish her," Junior whispered to Weasel, his voice laced with a dangerous edge. "I think she knows me. I remember her from Arlo's"

"Nah," Weasel replied, his tone dismissive.

"We ain't here for her. It's that kid we want. Let her go."

Junior bent down, got right in her face one last time. "You talk, you die. Your brother talks, he dies. That pretty boy Trevor talks, he dies. And it won't be quick. It'll be like Autumn—slow, scared, begging." He smiled. "Maybe we'll even use the same gator."

Then they were gone. The door slammed. Sage lay on the couch, breathing in short, painful gasps. Everything hurt—her face, her ribs, her shoulder, her head. The apartment was too bright, the sunlight streaming through the windows like knives. Just when she thought she was drifting away, she felt her phone vibrating in her pocket. With every ounce of strength she could muster, she answered it.

"Sage? You aight? You been gone a while," Antoine's voice crackled through the line.

"Antoine... Bryson...," she whimpered, the words catching in her throat. "Apartment... I'm sorry..."

The line went dead.

Back at the trailer, Antoine and Bryson exchanged a look of pure terror. "She's at the apartment," Antoine said, his voice cramped with dread.

"What the fuck bruh!" Bryson cursed. "I knew something was wrong."

They didn't waste another second. Antoine got his keys, and they jumped into his car, the tires squealing as they sped away. Antoine drove like the devil was chasing him. They raced down Rivette's Backbone Road. They knew, in their guts, that they were already too late.

"Faster," Bryson commanded.

"I'm doing eighty in a forty." But Antoine pressed harder on the gas. The truck's engine screamed.

Chapter 22-Sage, Bryson & Antoine

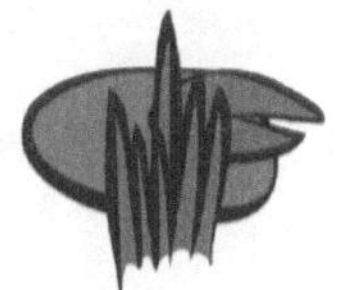

They reached the apartment in twelve minutes flat. The Impala's tires chewed the asphalt as Antoine slammed to a stop. It was early, but the gnawing feeling in Antoine's gut had driven them back to Sage's. The frantic call they'd gotten from Sage had been a jolt of pure, electric angst, and it still vibrated beneath their skin.

"There's her car," Bryson divulged, his eyes scanning the street. Sage's Honda Civic sat crookedly at the curb.

Antoine killed the engine. "Let's not jump to conclusions," he said, but the words felt hollow, even to his own ears. His hand instinctively went to the pistol tucked into the waistband of his jeans; the cold steel was comforting.

They moved fast, urgency propelling them up the stairs three at a time. The air in the hallway felt heavy, like it was holding its breath. Antoine knocked, his knuckles rapping sharply against the door. No answer. He knocked again, harder, his patience fraying.

"Sage? It's us! Open the door!"

Silence.

Bryson's hand went to the doorknob. He twisted it, it was unlocked.

The scene inside hit them like a punch to the gut.

Sage lay sprawled on the living room floor, amidst overturned furniture and scattered detritus. Her face was a swollen, bruised mess, one eye blackened shut, and a vicious gash marred her cheek. Dried blood caked her hair, and her breathing came in ragged, shallow gasps.

Bryson was on his knees in an instant, his hands gentle as he checked her pulse, felt for broken bones. "Sage? Sage, can you hear me?"

A weak moan escaped her lips, and her good eye fluttered open, focusing on Bryson with blurry recognition. "Bry... son..."

Antoine stood over her. His jaw clenched so tight the muscles jumped.

"Who did this? Who the hell did this?"

Sage coughed, a wet, rattling sound.

"They... they came... looking... looking for what we know...," Her voice was thin, each word an agonizing effort. "Said... said we were sticking our noses where... where they didn't belong..."

Bryson pressed a clean cloth he found in the kitchen to a gash on her forehead, his fingers careful, his touch as light as a feather.

"Who, Sage? Who were they?" badgered Antoine.

"Them... the men at the warehouse... They knew... knew we saw...," Pain flashed across her face, and she gasped, her body trembling. "Warned me... warned us... to stay away..."

Antoine's eyes burned with a furious fire.

"They touched my sister. Look at your fucking face! They messed with the wrong family. We gotta get you to the hospital."

"No... Antoine... they said... no hospital...," Sage's voice was barely audible. "Said... wouldn't be... safe..."

Bryson looked up. "She's right. Not right now. Not if they're watching." He ran an eye over her injuries, assessing with practiced detachment, despite the fury churning inside him.

"She needs stitches. She needs a doctor. But... not like this. Not where they can see her." He knew he could patch her up, keep her stable, but she needed more.

"I'm just a LPN, I'll see what I can do," said Bryson.

Antoine's hand tightened around the pistol.

"Okay, do what you need to do. I'm going back to that goddamn warehouse."

"Antoine, wait!" Bryson pleaded, his voice urgent. "Don't do nothin' stupid. Not yet. We need to think."

"Think!?" Antoine snapped. "My sister is lying there, beaten to a pulp and you want me to think!? They murdered your fucking sister! They think they can walk all over us like this? They have another thing coming."

"Aight I'll take care of yo' sister. But you... you need to be careful woe. We on't know who we dealing with. We on't know how many of 'em out there."

Antoine looked at Sage, his anger giving way to a flash of raw concern. "I'll be careful. But I'm coming back, and when I do, we finishin' this," he walked toward the door, then paused, turning back to Bryson. "Keep her safe. I swear, if anything else happens to her, I'll never forgive myself," he disappeared into the morning light.

Bryson knelt beside Sage, his touch gentle, his eyes filled with fierce protectiveness. "It's okay, Sage. I'm here. I won't let anything else happen to you."

He looked all over the apartment until he found a first aid kit. It was propped up against the wall in the pantry.

He worked quickly, efficiently, cleaning her wounds, bandaging the cuts, checking for any sign of serious injury. He spoke softly, soothingly, his voice, a calming presence amid the chaos. Sage's pain was clear, but she was strong. She didn't scream or make any noise other than a little hiss of air here and there.

As the adrenaline began to ebb, a different kind of aura filled the air. Bryson looked at Sage's battered face, at the strength that still flickered in her good eye. He saw not just the injured woman before him, but the fighter, the dreamer, the soul that burned so fiercely beneath the surface.

"I messed this up," she whispered, her voice still weak, but filled with self-reproach.

"No," Bryson said firmly, shaking his head. "You ain't do nothin' wrong. They were lookin' for us. It would have happened regardless," his hand brushed against her cheek, his touch feather-light. "You gon' be alright, Sage."

"Thank you... for staying," she sniffed, her eyes locked with his. There was something in her eyes, something more than gratitude, something that made his heart skip a beat.

The apartment fell silent; the only sound was the gentle rhythm of their breaths. The room filled with an unspoken energy, a raw, intimate vulnerability that transcended the pain and the fear.

"You know," Sage said softly, her voice barely above a whisper. "I always thought you were... strong. But I didn't know you were... gentle. Like this."

Bryson's breath caught in his throat.

"I... I try to be," he shifted closer, his gaze lingering on the curve of her lips. "You're strong too, Sage. Stronger than you know."

"I was scared," she admitted, her voice trembling. "So scared."

"It's okay to be scared," Bryson affirmed, his hand moving to cup her cheek. His thumb gently traced the line of her jaw, his touch galvanic.

"It's okay to let someone take care of you."

He leaned in, his breath warm against her skin. His lips brushed against hers, a tentative, hesitant touch that quickly deepened into something more. The kiss was slow, tender, filled with a mixture of longing and relief. A kiss that spoke of shared pain and shared strength, of a connection that had been forged in the fires of adversity.

"We shouldn't be doing this, Sage. Look at your face. Look at your eyes. You don't look too good. I'm just tryna make sure you heal and get better," said Bryson reluctantly.

Sage's hand moved to his hair, her fingers threading through his dark curls.

"Trust me. This'll make me feel much better."

She pulled him closer, her body pressing against him, the pain a dull throb in the background, overshadowed by the warmth of his caress. The kiss grew more urgent, more demanding, fueled by a desperate need for connection, for reassurance, for something real and tangible during the nightmare.

He lifted her into his arms, his movements careful but strong, and carried her to the bedroom. He laid her gently on the bed, his eyes never leaving hers. They undressed each other slowly, their hands exploring tenderness and reverence. Every touch was an affirmation, a silent reminder that they were both still there, still alive, still capable of feeling.

Their lovemaking was not about passion alone; it was about healing, about finding solace in each other's arms. It was about reclaiming their bodies, their agency, their right to feel pleasure in the face of violence that sought to strip it away. Every stroke was a silent promise, every sigh a shared release. They moved together with a slow, deliberate tempo, their bodies finding harmony that echoed the unspoken connection between their souls. The room was filled with the soft sounds of their shared intimacy, the quiet gasps and whispered reassurances weaving a fragile peace in the aftermath of chaos. It was in that shared vulnerability, in the delicate dance of their bodies, that they found a moment of respite, a brief sanctuary from the storm that raged outside.

Afterward, they lay tangled in the sheets. Sage nestled against Bryson, her head resting on his chest, the cadence of his heartbeat a soothing balm. The events of the past hours, the horror, the fear, the raw vulnerability all faded into the background, replaced by a profound sense of peace and connection. They held each other close, two souls seeking solace in the aftermath of trauma, finding a fragile, beautiful intimacy amidst the wreckage.

"Antoine said he messed up badly back then," Bryson finally ventured. "What did he mean?"

Sage took a slow breath, then another. "It's... it's a long story," she picked at a loose thread on the sheet. "And it ain't a pretty one either.

"We got time," Bryson said gently.

She gave a small giggle.

"Yeah, we got plenty of that. Alright. Fine. Look, Antoine... he wasn't always like this, you know? All... guarded and edgy. He used to be... bright. Full of energy. He was an artist, even back then. Always sketchin', paintin'. Had these wild dreams of moving to New York, opening a gallery."

"So, what happened?"

Sage's eyes drifted to the sun-riddled window.

"He got mixed up with the wrong crowd. Guys who dealt stuff. Coke, mostly. Antoine wasn't a dealer himself, not really. But he knew them, hung out with them. He thought he was... invincible, I guess. Thought he could play around the edges without getting burned."

"And he got burned?" Bryson guessed.

"Burned to a crisp," Sage said darkly. "One night, there was a fight. A bad one. Over money, over territory, the usual crap. Antoine... he got caught in the middle. Someone pulled out a knife. Things got ugly. Real ugly."

"He got stabbed?"

"Worse," Sage said quietly. "He... he used the knife. Tried to defend himself. And the other guy... he got stabbed. Badly. He was on life-support. The guy almost ain't make it. They said it was attempted murder."

Bryson's eyes widened. "Attempted murder? Dang."

"Yeah. Antoine swore it was self-defense. That he never meant to hurt the guy that bad. But... the other guys, his so-called friends, they all ratted on him. They said Antoine was the aggressor."

"That's why he went to prison?"

Sage nodded. "Yeah. Arrendale. His lawyer told him to take a plea deal. Three years. Three years of hell," she shivered, even though she wasn't cold.

"I visited him a few times each week. It changed him. Broke something inside him. All that... hope... it just... flickered out."

"That's tough," Bryson said softly.

"Tough ain't the word for it," Sage said. "I saw the way they looked at him. Like he was nothing. Like his life didn't matter," her voice wavered, and she took a moment to compose herself. "But you know what? He survived. He got through it. Maybe it changed him, but it didn't break him. He came out... different. Harder, maybe. But he came out."

"How'd he get out early?"

"Good behavior," Sage replied. "And... I pulled a few strings. Called some lawyers. It wasn't easy. But I wasn't 'bout to let him rot in there any longer than he had to. I knew he wasn't the person they made him out to be. He made a terrible mistake, but he wasn't a killer."

"You helped him out?"

"I did," Sage reiterated. "He had nowhere to go when he got out. No one wanted to hire an ex-con. So, he came to me. I let him crash on my couch. Helped him find odd jobs. I tried to remind him of who he used to be," she smiled faintly. "It wasn't always pretty. There were... rough patches. Times when I thought he was going to slip back into that old life. But... he didn't. He fought. He's still fighting."

"He's lucky to have you," Bryson said.

Sage shrugged. "He's my brother. We stick together. That's what family do," she looked at Bryson. "And that's why I know he'll help us. Because he knows what it's like to be on the outside, looking in. He knows what it's like to be judged, to be written off. He won't let that happen to Autumn."

Bryson nodded, understanding dawning in his eyes. "So, that's why he's so... willing to help?"

"Yeah," Sage said quietly. "That's why."

She took a deep breath, as if releasing a heavy weight. "He owes me, sure. But more than that, I think he owes himself. A chance to... make things right. In his own way."

Chapter 23- Sage, Bryson & Antoine

The soft glow of the table lamp did little to pierce the gloom that settled in Mrs. Hayes's living room. Bryson insisted they get out of Sage and Autumn's apartment before the men came back. They ended up at Mrs. Hayes' home. Sage lay on the couch, blanket pulled up to her chin. Her face was still a landscape of bruises and swollen flesh. Bryson sat beside her; his eyes fixed on her with a mixture of worry and simmering rage. Mrs. Hayes sat in her armchair, rosary beads clutched firmly in her hands, her lips moving in silent prayer.

Antoine stood by the window, staring out into the darkness. His fists were balled firmly at his sides. Bryson had seen that look before; it was the look Antoine got when his temper was about to snap.

"Th...This ain't right," Antoine stuttered, turning away from the window. His voice was rough with suppressed anger. "They can't just get away with this."

"We need to be smart, Antoine," Bryson advised, his voice quiet but firm. "Rushing in blind won't help. It'll just make things worse."

"Smart? How 'bout we go out to that warehouse and rip those bastards apart?" Antoine's voice grew louder, and he began pacing. "They hurt her, man. They could've killed her. For what?"

"For Trevor," Sage whispered, her voice hoarse. "For not giving them the answers they wanted." Her words were faint, but they hung heavily in the room.

Mrs. Hayes looked up, her eyes filled with silent strength. "Brysonito is right, Antoine. We must think before we act. We must not make things more dangerous."

"We will protect her now," Bryson added, standing up. He looked from Antoine to his mother to Sage. Antoine stopped pacing and ran a hand through his hair. "Protect her? They already got to her. They already proved we can't protect her."

Just then, a small figure emerged from the hallway, rubbing sleep from his eyes. It was Gabriel clutching a tattered teddy bear. His eyes, bright and innocent, bounced between the adults, a soundless question in their depths. He was too young to understand the gravity of the situation.

He shuffled over to Mrs. Hayes, burying his face in her skirt. "Abuela," he whispered, his tiny voice filled with sleep. "Where's Mommy?"

Mrs. Hayes's expression allayed in an instant. She reached down and scooped him up, settled him in her lap. "Shh, mijo," her tone softened, stroking his hair. "Tu madre is just sleeping. She'll be okay."

Gabriel looked at Sage with a slight frown. "Momma sleep a long time," he said, his small voice carrying a note of worry.

Sage's heart clenched. She reached out, gently touching Gabriel's arm.

"She's just very tired, sweetheart," she said, her voice reassuring. "She'll wake up soon."

Antoine's anger seemed to dissipate slightly at the sight of Gabriel. He crossed his arms. The presence of the child served as a reminder of what they were fighting for, of what was truly at stake. This wasn't just about revenge; it was about protecting the innocent, about ensuring that Gabriel didn't lose another person he loved.

Sage stirred slightly, her forehead wrinkled.

"I... I think I saw someone. Before... before it all went dark."

Everyone in the room leaned in, their attention focused on her.

"Who?" Bryson asked, urgently.

Sage's words caught in her throat. "One of them... he looked familiar. Like one of Arlo's buddies—my ex, remember?"

Antoine's face shifted. He knew about Arlo and how he abused his sister.

"Arlo? That piece of shit?" Antoine's voice was menacing. "You sure?"

Sage nodded slowly. "Pretty sure. One of his buddies, I don't remember his name though." She squeezed her eyes shut as if trying to retrieve the memory. "I don' t remember but the other guy had one weird-looking eye. Like it drifted off into the distance. He kept staring at me while Arlo's friend was beating my ass."

"We can't go to the police," Bryson restated. "Not yet. Not until we know more. We involve twelve, and it becomes public record. They might get spooked and disappear."

"So, what? We just sit here and wait for them to come back?" Antoine asked.

"No," said Mrs. Hayes firmly. "We pray. We ask for guidance."

Bryson was agitated and it showed. "Mama..."

"You underestimate the power of prayer, Brysonito. It helps. We pray for the answers and for Sage's healing," Mrs. Hayes said, her voice unwavering. "But we also work. God helps those who help themselves."

Antoine sighed and paced again. "I'm ready to leave and go find them, find who did this. Y'all holding me back"

"And what? Fight them head on? Get yourself hurt, or worse?" Bryson asked, trying to be reasonable. "That isn't the plan right now. We work on getting info, we plan and then we move on that plan. We can't go in guns blazing."

"Then what do we do?" Antoine asked, looking around at all of them. "What's the plan?"

"First, we make sure Sage is okay," Bryson intoned, looking at her with concern. "Mama, is there anything else we can do for her? Anything else she needs?"

"I gave her tea and ice to help the swelling. Some cream to ease the pain. Now, she needs to rest. And time," Mrs. Hayes said, standing as she went to get more tea.

"We should take shifts watching her tonight," said Bryson.

"I'll take the last shift," Antoine volunteered immediately.

"Mama will take the first shift. I'll take over after her. If Sage has anything she needs during our shift she'll let us know," said Bryson.

As Mrs. Hayes bustled around, preparing more tea, Antoine pulled out his phone.

"I'm gon' call some people. See if I can find out anything about Arlo's friends."

"Be careful who you call," Bryson cautioned. "We don't want to bring any unwanted attention."

"I know," Antoine replied, his eyes fixed on his phone. "I just need to see what I can dig up."

Hours ticked by. Bryson sat beside the couch, watching Sage sleep. Mrs. Hayes returned with a fresh pot of tea and sat in her armchair, her rosary beads once again moving through her fingers. Antoine paced quietly, occasionally glancing at his phone.

Sage drifted in and out of sleep. She mumbled incoherently at times, her words lost in the haze of pain and exhaustion. But every so often, she would open her eyes and look around, her face searching for theirs. And each time, she found them there, watching over her, protecting her.

As the sun began to filter through the windows, Antoine stood up and stretched. "My shift's over. I'm gonna go out for a bit. Need to... clear my head."

"Be careful, Antoine," Bryson cautioned.

"I will," Antoine replied, his eyes hardening. "But I ain't gon just sit here"

As Antoine left, Bryson took his place beside Sage. He watched her sleeping face, his heart aching with a mixture of love and anger. He thought about what she had said about Arlo's friend, about the look in his eye. And he knew, with a growing certainty, that he had to find Arlo before they got to Trevor.

He looked at his mother, who was gently lifting the sleeping Gabriel to bring him to bed. Mrs. Hayes had taken it upon herself to become Gabriel's rock. He knew he could count on her.

"Hey, mama," he whispered. "I'll be back, keep an eye on Sage."

"Be careful mi amor, be careful."

Chapter 24- Bryson & Antoine

The clatter of loose tools in the back of Antoine's Ford F-150 rustled as he cut on the engine. They rumbled down the potholed road. The truck was a testament to years of hard work and minimal upkeep; rust bloomed on its fenders like a stubborn rash, and the once-blue paint had faded to a dusty grey. Yet, somehow, bless its soul, the AC still managed to pump out a weak, but refreshing, stream of cool air. Bryson appreciated it, a small mercy against the brutal Florida humidity that clung to everything like a second skin.

Antoine had made the tough call to leave his Impala behind. The men at the warehouse had likely seen it, making it too conspicuous. His truck, on the other hand, blended into the rural landscape of Oak-Haven like a weathered fence post. They needed to move incognito if they were going to find answers.

Inside the cab, the space smelled faintly of motor oil. But for Bryson, it felt like a sanctuary of sorts, a mobile command center in their desperate quest. He found himself observing Antoine, a man he was beginning to know beyond their shared pain. Antoine's hands, calloused and scarred, clutched the steering wheel with a steady confidence. He had a quiet intensity beneath the surface that Bryson recognized all too well. It was of someone who'd been pushed to the edge, someone who had nothing left to lose.

"You were inside for a while, right?" Antoine asked suddenly, not looking at Bryson.

Bryson nodded, the memory surfacing like a jagged piece of wreckage.

"Yeah, two years. Blue Onion State Penitentiary."

"Tough place," Antoine mentioned, his gaze still fixed on the road.

"Yeah, you could say that." Bryson leaned back, the vinyl seat protesting with a groan. He hadn't shared much about his time inside, but something about Antoine's quiet empathy loosened his tongue.

"You have no idea," Bryson said with a sigh. "It's like... they strip you down, try to make you less than human. Always watching, always testing. There's this whole... hierarchy. Everyone's trying to prove something, usually how tough they are."

Antoine grunted in understanding. "Everyone trying to survive. It's the law of the jungle there. He flicked his cigarette out the window, his laugh sharp and bitter. "Man, you know what prison does? Makes you watch your back. All them soft boys, pretending they straight 'til lights out. Sweet ahh. I ain't no punk, never was, never will be. Anybody came to me sideways in there, I handled mines quick."

He spat out the window. "All that sweet shit gets a man killed, you hear me? Better to die than bend over like some fag."

He didn't meet Bryson's eyes when he said it—like the words were armor, hammered out of fear.

Bryson stared out the windshield. "Yeah bruh, survival's a bitch in there. But all that hate? That'll kill you faster than any soft boy ever did."

He flicked his gaze over and met Antoine's hard stare. "Loneliness, though... that's the real killer. Feeling like you're screaming underwater. Nobody hears you," Bryson confided. He let the silence stretch, then shrugged. "Books kept me sane. And sometimes the talks did too. Under the blankets, after lights out—whispering about our lives before. Shit you'd never say out loud. Sometimes you just needed to know another man no matter his sexuality was listening, not looking to cut your throat. Sometimes that was the bravest thing."

Antoine shifted in his seat. He didn't spit again. He didn't say anything at all.

"Y'all boys ain't have late night talks?" probed Bryson.

Antoine nodded. "Yeah, I remember those late-night talks. Those were the only times it felt... real. Like you weren't just a number."

"And little things, like getting a clean sheet. Or finding a hidden pencil. It sounds dumb as fuck, but those small things, those little wins, reminded me I was still myself," Bryson added.

Antoine smiled faintly, a flicker of recognition in his eyes. "I get it. It's all about holding onto something, anything, to keep from losing yo'self completely."

"You know, people look at me now and think they know me. But they don't see the beginning. They wasn't with me shooting in the gym. They ain't see a house where the lights cut off every other month, or a fridge that stayed empty more often than not," said Antoine, as he shook his head slowly.

"My moms worked two jobs, and my pops... he wasn't around. I pretty much raised myself. No one ever asked how I was doing. No one ever listened. You grow up learning to keep everything inside, you feel me? Like feeling somethin' makes you weak," confided Antoine, in a reflective tone.

"When I ended up in there, I figured I'd just be another number. But it was weird... I found something. Not peace exactly, but—connection. There's this bond, this strange kind of brotherhood. We've all been through the trenches in different ways, and somehow that brings us closer. It ain't freedom, but it's something," added Antoine.

Bryson shook his head in agreement. A few seconds passed before Antoine changed the subject.

"You ever wondered why you and Autumn look so different?"

Bryson chuckled, a dry, humorless sound.

"All the time, bruh. Especially growing up. People always thought I was adopted or somethin'. My moms Dominican. My dad—my real dad—he Black. Autumn's dad was different... white boy. He ain't stick around long after Autumn was born though. When that fell apart, moms went back to my father."

Antoine nodded slowly. "That ain't get weird?"

Bryson shrugged.

"Yeah, sometimes. But it worked—until it didn't. My dad... he died. Outta nowhere. One day he's there, the next, gone. It was his second stroke in two years. The doctor said he had high blood pressure and high cholesterol. The crazy thing is, he ain't e'en know he had high blood pressure until his first stroke. Pops ain't believe in going to the doctor. But I think the real reason is that he couldn't afford it. They told him to change his diet and gave him some pills to take daily. He took the pills but he was still eating that soul food. Fried chicken, fries, macaroni and cheese. He thought all the other options the doctor suggested were bland and ain't have no seasoning. He had called it while folks food. He wasn't going for it. Not gon' lie that shit fucked me, man. Had me geeked. I ain't e'en know how to process it. I just... fell."

"I get that. Grief can do that. It doesn't just break you—it changes your whole direction," related Antoine.

"I started messing up after that. Like I ain't care anymore. One bad choice turned into a hundred. That's how I ended up in prison. Never thought I'd be saying this shit out loud," said Bryson.

"Funny, isn't it? How easy it is to stay quiet out there... and how easy it is to talk in here."

Bryson flashed a faint smile. "Yeah. Maybe it's because someone finally gets it."

Antoine confirmed with a small grin.

"We heading to Arlo's place, right?" Bryson finally asked, trying to redirect the conversation to the reason for their drive.

"Yeah. Sage said one of the guys who roughed her up was Arlo's friend," Antoine disclosed.

They reached the outskirts of Oak-Haven, a rundown neighborhood that seemed to have been forgotten by time. Weathered bungalows with peeling paint-lined the streets. Antoine steered the truck down a side street, finally stopping in front of an apartment building. The building's façade was stained and cracked, and the windows were dark and vacant.

"This is it," Antoine annouced, cutting the ignition. He pulled out his handgun, checking the chamber. "Let's be careful. Arlo might not be alone."

They approached the building cautiously, their footsteps echoing in the stillness. Antoine rapped on the door with the butt of his gun, the sound sharp and insistent. There was no answer. He tried the knob, but the door was locked. He turned to Bryson with a smirk.

"Back door it is then."

They circled the building, their eyes scanning the windows for any sign of movement. As they reached the back, they saw a rickety set of metal stairs leading to the second floor. Antoine nodded, and they began to climb. At the top, they found a back door slightly ajar. Antoine pushed it open with the toe of his boot and stepped inside.

The apartment was dark and cramped. It was clear that Arlo lived in squalor. A threadbare mattress lay on the floor in the corner, and dirty clothes were strewn everywhere. As they searched the apartment, Bryson found a photo album tucked away in a drawer. He flipped through the pages, finding pictures of Arlo with a group of rough-looking men. One face stood out—a man with a shifty gaze and a distinctive scar across his cheek.

"Think this is Junior?" Bryson asked, showing the picture to Antoine.

Antoine studied the photo. "Could be. He looks like trouble."

Suddenly, they heard a noise from outside—a muffled thump, followed by the sound of footsteps running away. Antoine and Bryson exchanged a quick glance and bolted out the back door. They saw a person sprinting down the stairs, his silhouette outlined against the building.

"Arlo!" Antoine yelled, jumping down the stairs.

Bryson was faster. He anticipated Arlo trying to run to the back alley. He positioned his body and waited. Arlo jumped the last few steps. As Arlo landed, Bryson launched at the man, tackling him to the ground with a grunt. Arlo struggled, trying to break free, but Bryson held him down with brute force. Antoine was on them in seconds; his gun pointed at Arlo's head.

Antoine growled. "Where's the motherfuka who hurt my sister?"

Arlo's eyes expanded. He knew he was cornered.

"I... I don't know what you're talking about, man," he stammered, his voice twitchy.

Bryson tightened his grip. He slammed Arlo's head against the ground, once hard then again twice more. Arlo cried out in pain.

"Don't lie to us, Arlo," Bryson said, his voice hard. "Sage recognized him. She knows he was with you. Now, where is he?"

Antoine cocked the gun. The click was loud and clear. "Tell us, or I swear I'll blow your brains out right here."

Arlo's eyes darted between their faces, his resolve crumbling. "Okay! Okay! It was Junior! I told him to leave Sage alone, but he didn't listen!" he finally admitted.

"Where is he?" Antoine pressed the gun to Arlo's cheek. "Where can we find him?"

Arlo gave them an address and a name. A place on the other side of town, a neighborhood known for its drug activity.

"That's all I know, I swear!" Arlo pleaded.

Antoine pulled the trigger and shot Arlo in the thighs. Arlo screamed in pain.

"That's for putting your hands on my little sister. I'd put some more bullets in you but I gotta save em' for your lil' friends," Antoine said, his eyes cold. They didn't wait for Arlo to stop screaming. They left him there in a puddle of his blood.

They piled back into the pickup, Antoine behind the wheel. Bryson looked at his hands, stained with dirt and something else he didn't want to think about. He knew they had crossed a line, that they were moving further and further into dangerous territory. But he also knew that there was no turning back. They were committed now, driven by a need for justice that burned hotter than the Florida sun. They had a name and a place.

Chapter 25- Bryson & Antoine

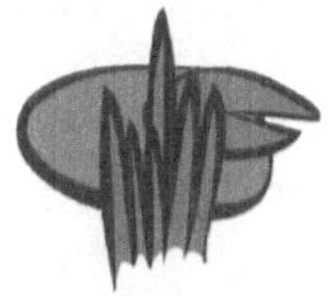

Antoine's truck grumbled. Rain lashed against the windshield, distorting the lines in the street. Bryson sat rigid, the .38 weighing in his jacket pocket.

"Almost there," Antoine warned, his gaze concentrated on the rain-slicked road. "Junior's place. Remember, we playin' this smart."

"Right," Bryson said, though his tone suggested anything but calm.

They turned onto a narrow road, lined with modest, single-story homes. Antoine slowed the truck, his eyes searching for a specific address.

"There," Bryson whispered, pointing to a house halfway down the block. As they approached, something caught Antoine's eye.

"Hold on," he instructed, slamming on the brakes. "See that?"

Two men were hauling something large and limp through the front door of the house. In the fleeting glimpse, Bryson recognized the tousled blond hair. Trevor.

"It's Trevor," Bryson pointed out, his voice tight. "They got him."

"And those two? Gotta be Junior and his homie," Antoine added.

"Homie?" Bryson said, narrowing his eyes. "As in, the guy who helped Junior beat up Sage in her apartment?"

Antoine nodded. "Yeah, it gotta be."

Antoine hesitated, his hand on the gear shift. Then, a sudden movement made him freeze. Weasel, his face pale, turned and looked directly at the truck. For a heart-stopping moment, their eyes met. Antoine held his breath, his body tense. Weasel stared for a beat, then, with a shrug, turned back and disappeared into the house.

"Fuck!" Antoine grumbled, letting out a slow breath. "He saw us."

"He didn't recognize the truck, right?" Bryson asked anxiously.

"Nahh," Antoine drawled, shaking his head. "I'm glad I left the Impala. Plus, he's a moron, he prolly just assumed it was someone taking a wrong turn."

"Still, too close," Bryson said. "We gotta get out of here."

Antoine agreed. He pulled away from the house, driving slowly, cautiously. He turned onto the next street, then another, circling back until they were a good quarter mile away. He parked the truck in a patch of dense brushes, hidden from the road.

"Alright," Bryson said. "Game time. What's the play?"

"We gotta get the jit outta there," Antoine stressed. "And we gotta get some answers from those two."

"Right," Bryson said. "But how? They've got Trevor inside. They'll be expecting us."

"Then we don't come as expected," Antoine reasoned. He pulled the .45 from his waistband and checked the magazine. "We do it their way. But on our terms."

They went over the plan again, meticulously, covering every possibility, every angle. The rain continued to fall, a steady rhythm. When they were as ready as they could be, they stepped out of the truck, Antoine's .45 and Bryson's own smaller handgun cold in their hands.

They moved through the rain, using the trees and bushes for cover. The house came into view again. They approached cautiously, their footsteps silent on the wet ground.

Peeking through a window, they got a clear view into the living room. The sight made their blood run cold. Trevor was tied to a chair, his shirt ripped open, a gag stuffed in his mouth. Junior and Weasel stood over him, their faces hard, their movements rough. They saw Junior raise his hand and slap Trevor hard across the face.

"Bastards," Bryson sibilated.

They tried the back door, then the garage, but both were locked. Every window seemed sealed as well.

"We could break a window," Bryson whispered.

"Nahh," Antoine said. "Too noisy. Too messy. And it wouldn't work anyway. We gotta get them to open the door."

"So, what, we just knock?" Bryson asked, a hint of disbelief in his voice.

"Yeah," Antoine said, a smile spreading across his face. "Just like old friends dropping by."

Bryson took a deep breath, squared his shoulders, and ran to the front door. He pounded on it, three loud, insistent raps. From inside, they could hear voices, sharp and startled. Then, there was the sound of movement, footsteps approaching. Another slap echoed and Trevor whined from behind the gag.

"Who's that?" a voice yelled from inside. It was Junior.

"Some guy," Weasel responded with annoyance, walking towards the door.

The door creaked open, revealing Weasel, his face suspicious. "Whatcha want?" he questioned.

Bryson stepped closer, his voice calm, almost casual. "My car broke down," he lied. "Thought maybe you could help."

Weasel stared at him, his eyes tapered, then he let out a harsh, mocking chuckle. "Go fuck yourself," he objected, and started to close the door.

That was the cue. In a flash, Bryson moved. He grabbed Weasel's shirt collar, yanking him forward and slamming his head against the doorframe with brutal force. Weasel's eyes rolled back in his head, and he crumpled to the porch, unconscious.

Antoine was through the door in an instant, gun drawn. Junior stood in the living room, his eyes filled with shock, his hand reaching for the handgun in his waistband.

"Don't e'en think about it, pussy," Antoine growled, aiming the .45.

Junior froze, his hand hovering over his weapon. He looked from Antoine to Bryson, then to Trevor, his face a mask of disbelief.

"Wh...what the hell is this?" he stammered.

"It's payback," Bryson said, his voice cold. "And shits 'bout to get real messy."

They moved quickly, securing Junior, making sure he was disarmed. Then, they rushed to Trevor. He was bound tightly to the chair, his face bruised and swollen. They quickly untied him, removing the gag from his mouth.

"Bryson?" Trevor quavered, his voice hoarse. "What's going on?"

"We're getting you out of here," Bryson said gently, his hand on his shoulder.

But then, Junior made his move. He lunged forward, catching Antoine off guard. They wrestled, a chaotic, desperate struggle, a tangle of limbs and curses. The gun went off with a deafening roar, the sound echoing in the small room. Junior clutched at his chest, his eyes wide with shock, then he collapsed to the floor, a dark stain spreading rapidly across his shirt.

Weasel moaned, stirring on the porch.

The room went deathly silent, the only sound was the heavy rain outside. Antoine stood there, chest heaving. The gun hung loosely in his hand.

"Sh..shit," he stuttered, staring at Junior's body.

"We ain't come here to murk him," Bryson surprised, his voice shaking.

"He attacked me," Antoine said, his voice defensive. "It was self-defense."

Bryson nodded. "It's done now, dawg. We gotta move."

They quickly checked Weasel, who was still unconscious but breathing. Then, they turned to Trevor.

"What were they doing to you?" Bryson asked. "Why did they bring you here?"

Trevor looked at them. "They... they wanted to know what I told you. About the car. About the driver."

"And why were they so interested?" Bryson pressed.

Trevor hesitated, then he blurted out, "I don't know! They just... they kept asking the same questions. Over and over."

Antoine knelt, his eyes hard. "Trevor, think hard. Did they say anything else? Anything at all?"

"One of them... that guy outside on the porch... he said... he said I should have kept my fuckin' mouth shut. He said Autumn should have too."

"About what?" Antoine pressed.

"He didn't say. He just said she... she messed with the wrong people."

"Who are the wrong people?" Bryson demanded.

Weasel moaned again and opened his eyes. He looked around, confused, then he saw Junior's lifeless body on the ground.

"Fuck!" He screamed. "What did you guys do to him." He got up quickly and went towards the kitchen. He opened all the drawers rummaging through it. Then he pulled a knife from the drawer and ran back to Antoine with the knife in his hand.

"You killed him!" Weasel yelled. "You killed Junior!"

Antoine stood his ground. "He came at me. I defended myself."

"You murdered him!" Weasel screamed, advancing towards Antoine with the knife.

Antoine dodged Weasel's swing while Bryson pushed him into the wall. The knife fell from his hand and skated over to Trevor's foot.

"He killed Junior!" Weasel yelled. He lunged at Antoine, attempting to get around Bryson. Bryson yanked Weasel's arm, twisting it behind his back. Antoine moved in quickly and stomped on the knife.

"You wanna die too," Antoine barked. "We have bigger problems right now."

Weasel, now disarmed and restrained, glared at Antoine, hatred burning in his eyes. "You ain't seen the last of this."

Trevor looked at Weasel, then at Junior's lifeless body. Everything had spiraled out of control so quickly.

"Aiight fuck," Bryson said. "We need to focus. Why did you and yo' friend kill Autumn? Who ordered it?"

Weasel spat on the floor. "I ain't tellin' y'all shit!"

Antoine grabbed Weasel by the collar, yanking him close. "You listen to me, you little weasel. You're going to tell us everything. Or I'll make you wish you were dead."

Weasel hesitated, fear flickering in his eyes. He knew Antoine wasn't bluffing. He let out a shaky breath.

"Autumn... she messed with the wrong people," Weasel recounted, his voice trembling. "She stuck her nose into somethin' she shouldn't have."

"What the fuck is that somethin'?" Antoine pressed, his voice urgent.

"That...that the president of the university was selling dope," Weasel spilled. "She had proof. She was gon' expose him. They warned her to stay quiet, but she wouldn't listen."

"Who warned her?" Bryson challenged.

"I'ont know...the president's people?" Weasel responded with uncertainty. "They told her if she said anythin' they would kill her. She ain't listen, so they killed her."

"So, the president of the university ordered her to be killed?" Antoine restated. Weasel shook his head, tears welling up in his eyes.

"Who killed her?" Bryson asked, his voice hard. "Who pulled the trigger?"

Weasel hesitated again, his eyes darting around the room. "I... I don't know exactly. Bugsy... Bugsy knows more than me. He's the one who handles things. He has a close relationship with the president. I just work for Bugsy; he only tells us what he wants us to know."

"Bugsy?" Antoine said, his voice dangerous. "Where can we find him?"

"He... he has a warehouse," Weasel stammered, his voice barely audible. "On the edge of town. Near the old docks."

Antoine released Weasel, who slumped to the floor, sobbing quietly. Bryson looked at Antoine, then at Trevor.

"We gon' find Bugsy," Bryson said, his voice firm. "And we gon' get the truth."

"What about him?" Trevor asked, gesturing to Weasel.

"We can't just leave him here," Bryson contributed.

Antoine looked down at Weasel, then back at the others.

"Nahh," he agreed, "But we ain't got no time to tie his ass up and drag him to the swamp. He'll be fine here next to his friend. He won't snitch, there's prolly a warrant out for his arrest anyways."

Antoine grabbed his gun from the floor, double-checking the magazine. "Let's go. We have a warehouse to find."

They stepped out into the pouring rain, leaving Weasel in the house with his deceased roommate. They hopped into the F-150 and screeched off.

Chapter 26-Trevor, Bryson & Antoine

The gray light of a stormy day made everything look dull. Bryson reclined in the passenger seat. Trevor sat stiff in the back. He looked uncomfortable. Antoine was driving.

"Okay, Trevor," Bryson started, trying to keep his voice calm. "Tell us everythin' Autumn told you about that college president and his... side business."

Trevor shifted, rubbing his hands on his jeans. Rain water dripping from his hair.

"It... it started a few months ago. Look, it wasn't one big moment where everything clicked. It was small things at first. Autumn had this work-study gig at the university, helping in the central supply depot. Basically, they'd get all kinds of stuff for the labs, dorms, even the administrative offices. She was good with details, always noticed if something was out of place. Then one day she found something weird with the orders they were getting."

"Weird how, jit?" Antoine asked, keeping his eyes on the road.

"Like, they were getting way too much stuff. Like, big orders of certain chemicals—stuff that should've lasted months, but they were getting deliveries weekly. And not from the usual suppliers. These were... shell companies, she called them. Names that sounded made up. Then... then she started digging, y'know, doing her own research online."

Autumn had eyed the crate marked *Office Supplies*—too heavy, taped up twice. Later, at her laptop, a half-dozen browser tabs glared with anonymous LLCs and PO Boxes. Her fingers hovered over the keyboard, heart stuttering at the thought: *What if I'm already seen?*

"At first she found barely anything about them. No real websites, no real addresses. Just a couple of PO boxes or weird phone numbers that led nowhere," Trevor glanced between them. "And then she found out... they were hiding things in those orders."

"Hiding what?" Antoine wondered.

"Drugs. She'd find boxes labeled *paper* that would be incredibly heavy. So, she got curious, and one night, after her shift, she peeked inside a couple of them. That's when she found the drugs. Stashed inside seemingly ordinary packages, like those thick shipping catalogs but the centers were dug out, and resealed. Or inside boxes with those foam packing peanuts, underneath was bundles of white powder," Trevor took a deep breath.

There was a quiet moment, just the sound of the rain. Bryson looked at Antoine. This was bigger than they thought.

"She tried to talk to a couple of other people who worked in the same department. They told her to ignore it, that things like this was none of her business. One of them even gave her a real creepy vibe, like he knew more than he was letting on and was warning her. That's when she really freaked out. She realized how dangerous this was. She thought about quitting the job, just walking away, but she felt like she couldn't. That she had to do somethin'," added Trevor.

"How did the president find out she knew?" Bryson asked carefully.

"She told someone at the school," Trevor said, looking down. "A professor she trusted. But that professor ratted her out to the president, trying to get on his good side, or somethin'."

"That's green," Antoine chimed in.

"Nahh forreal. Then Autumn found out she'd been ratted out, but it was too late. They already knew she was poking around." Trevor's voice got quieter. "And that's when she changed. She got scared. She told me to stop asking questions. Said she was trying to keep me safe. She was always looking over her shoulder." He looked at Bryson. "That's why we broke up. I thought she was being crazy."

"She told me," Trevor went on. "The day before... she died. She said they knew she told me about them when they went through her phone. Said the President would rather get rid of her than get busted."

"This President," Antoine said. "What's his name?"

Trevor hesitated, looking really scared.

"President Sterling."

Bryson gave a short, dry laugh. "Sterling. Good name for a big-time dealer, huh?"

The drug operation wasn't some small-time college campus hustle; it was a sophisticated, multi-layered network stretching far beyond Oak-Haven. They specialized in cocaine and synthetic opioid, highly addictive and incredibly lucrative, shipped in disguised consignments to the university's research labs. President Sterling wasn't just turning a blind eye; he was deeply involved. His motivation stemmed from a confluence of factors: a crippling gambling debt, a desire to secure a legacy through a massive new university building project, and a misplaced sense of invincibility. He used his influence to manipulate university finances. Funneling funds through shell corporations and laundering drug money as research grants and endowment contributions.

He coerced some staff and students into aiding the operation, either through threats or promises of advancement, and ruthlessly shushed anyone who stumbled too close to the truth. He saw himself not as a criminal, but as a visionary, believing the ends justified the means. In his twisted view, a few lives lost were a small price to pay for the progress he envisioned for the university. What began as a risky venture to solve his personal problems quickly became a twisted obsession with power and control, with him convincing himself that he was untouchable.

"He's not just some small-time guy," Trevor said, his voice shaking a little. "He's got power. This is his whole thing, not just a side gig."

"And we just stepped right into it," Antoine said with a smile. He looked at Trevor. "You're in this now, jit. Deep. You saw a guy get killed, and you know too much."

Trevor looked like he was about to throw up. He was trapped, and he knew it.

"You on't say a word about this to anyone. You hear me?" Antoine beseeched. "You with us now."

Bryson nodded. "We stick together."

Trevor's shoulders slumped. He had no choice. "Okay," he said quietly. "Okay, I'm in."

They started talking about what to do next.

"Bugsy's warehouse," Bryson said. "That's where we go first."

"That's where they keep stuff, and maybe the money," Antoine said.

"We gotta get some info first," Bryson said. "We can't just walk in."

Trevor spoke up. "Maybe I can help. I know things. Y'know, things from Autumn."

"What kind of things?" Antoine asked.

"About the warehouse. Who goes there. What they do." Trevor hesitated. "I know a guy who does deliveries there. He goes to a lot of places. He might know somethin'."

"Can you talk to him?" Bryson asked.

"Maybe," Trevor said. "But I can't tell him why I'm asking. He'll get all weird."

"Just be smart jit," Antoine instructed. "We need info, but we don't want to make anyone suspicious."

They kept talking, trying to figure everything out. They went over every little thing Trevor had said, and every idea they had. They were all feeling a little more sure of themselves, like they were a team now.

They were going to the warehouse. Bugsy's place. Where the answers might be. It was going to be dangerous, but they were ready.

Chapter 27- Trevor, Bryson & Antoine

Trevor sat in the back of the pickup, staring at his phone. He wasn't just thinking about making the call to Skip; he was remembering specific details about Autumn's behavior in the weeks before her death. One evening, he recalled, she had hastily shut her laptop when he entered their apartment. Another time, he overheard her having a hushed, anxious phone conversation. Now, piecing everything together, he realized she had been living in fear, gathering information in secret.

He scrolled through his contacts, his finger hovering over Skip's name. This was it. This call, this conversation, could be the key that unlocked everything or the mistake that landed them all in a deeper hole. He pressed the call button, the phone ringing in his hand feeling heavy as a brick.

"Come on, Skip, pick up," he muttered under his breath, his gaze flicking up to Antoine and Bryson in the rearview mirror.

The phone rang twice before a gruff voice answered. "Yeah?"

"Hey, it's... it's me, Trevor." He hated how his voice sounded, all high and shaky.

"Trevor? What up! I wasn't expecting a phone call from you."

"I know, I know. I just, uh, had a question. Something came up." He hoped his vague answer was enough. He couldn't risk saying anything outright.

"A question? You called me in the middle of dinner with my family for a damn question?" The voice on the other end was laced with annoyance.

"Just... just about the warehouse. The one on the old docks."

A pause. Then, a wary, "What about it?"

"Just... they still getting deliveries at all hours? Or is there, like, a schedule?"

"Schedule?" The guy snorted. "Things happen when they happen. Could be noon, could be midnight. Depends on what they need, when they need it. Why you askin'?"

Trevor swallowed hard. "Just… curious. Thinking about picking up some extra work. Driver or something. Y'know."

Another pause, longer this time. Trevor held his breath. "Look, Trev," the voice finally said, "I ain't got time for your games. If you're looking for a job, fill out the damn application. If you got somethin' else on your mind, spit it out."

"No, no, that's it. Just curious about the deliveries. Thanks, man. 'preciate it."

Trevor hung up before the guy could say anything else. His heart hammered against his ribs.

"Well?" Bryson asked, his eyes intense.

"I got somethin'," Trevor said, trying to sound more confident than he felt. "Guy said there's no real schedule. Deliveries come in whenever they're needed. Could be any time."

"Any time, huh?" Antoine mused, tapping his fingers on the steering wheel. "That's something. But ain't enough."

"He also said… he said there's cameras all around the outside. On the fence, the gate, everywhere."

"Surveillance cameras?" Bryson said, nodding. "Figures."

"So how we gonna get past them?" Antoine asked.

Trevor took a deep breath. "I got an idea. It's a bit... out there. But it might work."

"Spit it out, jit," demanded Antoine.

"Okay, so, here's what I was thinking," he began, his voice a little faster than usual. "We know they got cameras, right? And a guard at the gate. So, we can't just roll up and expect to get in. But... what if we distract them?"

Antoine leaned forward. "Distract them how?"

"Well," Trevor said, trying to sound confident, "I could go first. I'll take the van, like I'm making a delivery or something. I'll tell them I'm late, or they got the time wrong. Something to get them to open the gate."

Bryson raised an eyebrow. "And then what? We magically teleport inside?"

"No, no, hear me out," Trevor insisted, his voice picking up speed. "While I'm at the gate, you two hide in the back of the van. Under some blankets, or whatever we can find. I'll drive through, get past the guard, and then once we're inside, y'all can slip out."

Antoine tapped his fingers on the steering wheel. "So, you're the decoy."

"Yeah! Yeah, exactly!" Trevor said, relieved that Antoine seemed to be getting it. "I'll keep the guard busy, try to keep their attention on me. And while they're focused on me, you guys slip past them without them knowing," Trevor explains further, adding detail to it. "It will work because then they won't be able to know who we really are."

Bryson shook his head slowly. "That's fucking risky, Trevor. What if the guard wants to check the back of the van? What if they ask too many questions?"

"We'll just have to make sure they don't," Trevor said,with a little more conviction than he felt. "I'll... I'll come up with some excuses. Say it's fragile equipment, or it's sealed, or... I don't know. I'll think of somethin'. We'll time it right."

"Timing?" Antoine asked.

"Yeah, timing! If we move quick, then we'll be good." Trevor explained.

Trevor continued with details.

"We gotta move when the gate opens, we gotta move fast. Y'all gon' wait a couple of minutes after I pass the guard house before y'all get out and move towards the warehouse. This will give the guard a little time to relax. Also, if we do this around eight or nine at night then it's darker and the guard house won't be able to see y'all clearly when y'all get out of the van. If anything, we'll knock out the lights in the back of the van."

Antoine considered the plan, chewing on the inside of his cheek. "And what happens once we're inside?"

Trevor shrugged. "That's where things get tricky. But at least we'll get past the gate, past the cameras. We just need to distract them long enough." Trevor went over the details again for a couple more minutes.

"Okay," Antoine finally said. "It's risky. But it might just be crazy enough to work."

They knew they couldn't roll up to the warehouse in his beat-up pickup. It wouldn't look right. Too conspicuous. They needed a legitimate-looking delivery vehicle.

"I know a guy," Antoine finally said, a slow grin spreading across his face. "Runs a small moving company. Owes me a favor." A quick call, a bit of persuasive talking, and soon they were parked a few blocks away from the warehouse, the keys to a nondescript white panel van jingling in Antoine's hand.

They loaded the back with some old moving boxes from the moving company to make it look more authentic. Now, all they had to do was make it through the gate.

They spent the next hour refining the plan, going over every detail, every possible complication. They checked their gear, making sure their weapons were ready. Trevor felt a knot of fear tightening in his stomach, but beneath it, there was a strange sense of exhilaration. This was it. This was how they were going to get to Bugsy.

The rain had slowed to a drizzle by the time they were ready. Trevor drove the van towards the warehouse. They were all wearing dark clothes. Antoine and Bryson both got into the back of the van and covered themselves with some moving boxes, while Trevor made his way towards the gate.

Trevor approached the gate, his heart pounding. The floodlights illuminated the area, making him feel like he was on a stage. He stopped in front of the intercom and took deep breath.

"Go ahead," a voice crackled through the speaker.

Trevor cleared his throat. "Delivery for... uh, for Mr. Bugsy," Trevor stammered, trying to keep his voice steady. "Got some... some equipment he ordered."

There was a long pause. "Delivery? At this hour? Nobody told me about any delivery."

"It's... it's a rush job," Trevor clarified, sticking to the lie. "Mr. Bugsy said it had to be here tonight. Top priority. Check your list. Should be there." Trevor's heart hammered so hard he worried the guard could hear it through the speaker.

Another pause. Trevor's hand drifted toward the gear shift, ready to throw it in reverse and gun it.

Then—with a reluctant sigh, the gate buzzed open. Trevor pulled the van forward, careful to drive slowly, his eyes moving everywhere, taking in the security cameras mounted on the fence. He didn't see any that moved so he assumed that they were on constant recording and not being manually controlled.

As he pulled up to the guard booth, a man in a dark uniform stepped out, a flashlight in his hand. He eyed Trevor with suspicion.

"You're late," the guard said, his voice low and hard. "And I wasn't expecting you."

"Yeah, well, things got held up," Trevor said, doing his best to look casual. "Mr. Bugsy wanted this stuff tonight, no matter what. I just do what I'm told."

The guard shined the flashlight into the back of the van, momentarily illuminating the boxes. Trevor's heart leaped into his throat. He held his breath, praying that Antoine and Bryson were completely hidden. The guard peered inside for a few seconds, then looked back at Trevor.

"What's in the boxes?" he asked.

"Equipment. Y'know, for the... the business," Trevor said, trying to sound vague. "I don't really ask questions. I just deliver."

The guard stared at him for another long moment, then finally stepped aside.

"Alright, alright. Just park it over there, by the loading dock. And make it quick."

Trevor nodded, forcing a smile, and pulled the van forward. He drove through, tires crunching on gravel. The warehouse was bigger than he'd imagined—a sprawling concrete beast with small, high windows that revealed nothing. Two other vehicles sat in the lot: a black SUV with tinted windows and a beat-up sedan missing its front bumper.

He found the designated delivery parking area and stopped the vehicle. He waited a few moments, then gave a quick, subtle tap on the wall of the cab. Antoine and Bryson stirred to life and opened the back of the van just a crack.

Antoine and Bryson slipped out of the back of the van. They were both armed. They told Trevor to stay in the vehicle. Trevor didn't argue. He watched as they cautiously made their way towards the warehouse, their figures disappearing into the night.

Chapter 28- Bryson, Antoine, Trevor & Bugsy

The warehouse was large and imposing, a dark shape against the night sky. Trevor could hear the faint thumping of music from inside, a dense bass that vibrated through the air. He checked his watch. It had only been a few minutes.

Suddenly, he heard a faint shout, followed by the unmistakable sound of breaking glass. Trevor's heart hammered.

Antoine and Bryson moved with stealth, sticking to the shadows as they approached the warehouse. As they got closer, the music grew louder, a pounding rhythm that vibrated through the ground. They heard women laughing.

Antoine signaled to Bryson to wait. He then cautiously peered through a grimy window. What he saw made him freeze for a second. Inside, a makeshift party was in full swing. A group of men, three of them, sat around a table, drinking and smoking cigars. Four women were dancing, their movements unrestrained. Dollar bills fluttered through the air, raining down on the dancers.

Bryson peeked over Antoine's shoulder. "Well, I would hate to ruin the party," he marveled, an amusement in his voice.

"We ain't come here to play nice," Antoine responded. "We're the party crashers."

They checked the door, finding it locked, but an adjacent window was slightly ajar. With a silent nod, Antoine pushed the window open just enough to slip through. Bryson followed, and they found themselves inside a dimly lit storage area, crates stacked high around them. The music was deafening now, shaking the walls.

They slowly moved towards the sound, their steps silent on the concrete floor. They passed through a narrow doorway and into a large, open space.

Antoine and Bryson exchanged a glance. This was it. There was no turning back. With another silent nod,

Antoine stepped forward, his hand on the gun at his hip. He looked at Bryson and mouthed the words, "Let's go."

The sound of the music and the women' laughter drowned out their footsteps as they approached the main room. They moved quietly behind a stack of crates, their eyes taking in the scene. The bass-laded track that vibrated in their chests.

"Well, this party... is jumpin'," Bryson emphasized, his voice barely audible over the music.

"More like a goddang circus," Antoine sputtered back. "Stay close."

They moved slowly along the edge of the room, trying to remain unnoticed. The scene was chaotic, distracting, which was both good and bad. Good because they were less likely to be seen, bad because it was harder to assess the situation and find Bugsy.

"There," Bryson whispered, pointing to a doorway at the far end of the room. "Looks like it leads to another part of the building."

Antoine nodded. "Let's check it out. Maybe we'll find something more... useful."

They made their way towards the doorway. No one paid them any mind, their attention focused entirely on the spectacle in front of them. As they reached the doorway, Antoine paused, pressing his ear against the wall.

"Hear that?" he whispered.

Bryson listened. Faintly, over the music and the laughter, he could hear voices, deeper and more serious. "Sounds like talking," he said.

"Business talk," Antoine speculated.

He pushed the door open slowly, just a crack, and peeked into the next room. It was smaller and quieter, somberly lit by a single lamp on a desk. Two men sat at the desk, leaning over what looked like a ledger. A third man stood by the window, his back to them, smoking a cigarette.

"Bingo," Antoine whispered. "That one by the window. Gotta be Bugsy."

Bryson nodded. The man by the window was larger than the others, with a bald head and a broad back. He had an air of authority, even from a distance.

"What's the play?" Bryson asked.

"We go in," Antoine said, his voice rigid. "We ask some questions. And we get some answers."

"And if they on't wanna give us answers?" Bryson pressed.

Antoine grinned, a flash of teeth in the dim light. "Then we make 'em."

He pushed the door open wider and stepped into the room, Bryson right behind him. The sudden intrusion caused all three men to look up, startled. The music from the other room seemed to fade away as the tension in this room amplified to an extreme level.

"Well, well, well," Antoine went on, his voice casual, but his eyes sharp. "Looks like we crashed a private meeting. Hope we're not interrupting anything important."

The bald man—Bugsy—turned slowly. "Who the hell are you?" he growled.

"Just some concerned citizens," Antoine replied, stepping further into the room. "We're looking for some information. Thought maybe you could help us out."

"Information?" Bugsy repeated, his eyes narrowing. "About what?"

"About a girl," Bryson chimed in, stepping forward. "Autumn Hayes."

Bugsy's face hardened. One of the other men at the desk started to rise from his chair, but Bugsy held up a hand, stopping him.

"I don't know no Autumn Hayes," Bugsy replied, his voice monotoned, but a slight tension lined his face.

"Don't give us that bullshit," Antoine snapped. "We know you know her. We know what you do here. We know you were involved in her death."

Bugsy chuckled. "You think you can just walk in here and make accusations? You got some balls kid; I'll give you that. But you're in over your heads."

"Maybe," Bryson said. "But we're not leaving without answers."

"You're not leaving at all," Bugsy responded. He nodded to the two men at the desk, who both stood up, their hands disappearing beneath their jackets.

The atmosphere in the room turned electric. Antoine and Bryson knew they were outnumbered, but they were also prepared. They had come this far. They weren't about to back down now.

"We don't want any trouble," Antoine said, his hand hovering near the gun at his hip. "We just want to know who killed Autumn Hayes. Tell us, and we'll be on our way."

"Trouble?" Bugsy sneered. "You came looking for trouble. And you found it."

Suddenly, one of the men at the desk charged forward, pulling a knife from his jacket. Antoine reacted instantly, drawing his own weapon and firing a shot. The bullet hit the man in the shoulder, sending him stumbling back.

Bryson drew his gun, his eyes scanning the room. The third man, who had been by the window, now pulled out a pistol and aimed at Bryson. Bryson dove to the side, narrowly avoiding the shot. The bullet slammed into the wall behind him. The music from the other room stopped abruptly. Replaced by the sounds of shouting and confusion. The door to the party room burst open, and several more men poured into the room, their eyes wide with shock and alarm.

Antoine and Bryson found themselves surrounded, outnumbered and outgunned. But they were not afraid. They were ready to fight. And they were ready to die.

"We don't want to hurt anyone who doesn't deserve it," Bryson shouted, his voice cutting through the chaos. "But if you get in our way... you'll regret it."

Bugsy just laughed, a cruel sound. "You think you can take us all? You're insane."

The fight began. Guns fired, fists flew, and bodies crashed against the walls. Antoine and Bryson fought with desperate ferocity, fueled by rage and grief.

Antoine traded blows with one of Bugsy's men, his movements quick and precise. He disarmed the man, then slammed him against a table, knocking him unconscious. Bryson tackled another man, wrestling him to the ground, pinning him down with a brutal efficiency that surprised even himself.

Bugsy watched the scene unfold, his expression a mixture of anger and something else... something like respect. He pulled out his own gun, a large, heavy revolver, and aimed it at Bryson.

Just as he was about to fire, Antoine saw him and lunged forward, shoving Bugsy to the side. The shot went wild, smashing a lamp on the desk. Bugsy turned on Antoine, anger contorting his features.

"You want to play hero?" he snarled, swinging the revolver. "I'll show you what a hero looks like... in a coffin."

They grappled, their bodies colliding with a brutal force. Antoine fought with everything he had, every ounce of strength, every shred of determination. He had come here for Autumn, for Sage, for himself. He was not going to fail.

With a final, desperate move, Antoine twisted Bugsy's arm, forcing him to drop the gun. It clattered to the floor. They both went for it. Antoine got to it first, scooping it up just as Bugsy was about to get up.

He pointed the gun at Bugsy. They were face to face now.

"Tell me who killed her, and all this ends now," barked Antoine. "Tell me everything, and I'll let you walk."

Bugsy hesitated, his eyes drifting between Antoine and the gun. He knew he was beaten. He knew he had no choice. But he also knew that giving up this information was a death sentence. He knew that he had his own boss to contend with. He looked at Antoine, defeated.

"You got me," he faltered. "I'll tell you. But you gotta understand... it wasn't my call...I just... I follow orders." The bravado he'd carried moments before had completely evaporated.

"Orders from who?" Bryson pressed, stepping closer. His voice was low, but there was an edge to it that made Bugsy flinch. "Who told you to kill Autumn Hayes?"

Bugsy's lips twisted into a grimace. He glanced at the men scattered around the room, some still groaning, others slowly starting to get back to their feet. He let out a long, defeated sigh.

"It... it was the President," he finally disclosed. "President Sterling."

"Sterling ordered the hit?" Antoine asked. "Why? What did Autumn do?"

"She found out," Bugsy said, his voice still hushed. "She found out about... about everything. The drugs, the money laundering. She was going to expose him. He couldn't let that happen."

"So, he had her killed?" Bryson questioned, his voice filled with disgust. "Just like that?"

Bugsy nodded slowly. "He said it was... necessary. For the good of the... the business. He said she was a loose end, a threat. He said it had to be done."

"And you did it?" Antoine asked, riddled with contempt. "You just followed orders like some kind of... friggin' puppet?"

"I didn't... I didn't kill her myself," Bugsy said quickly, his eyes widening with fright. "I just... I made the arrangements. I hired someone. Someone who... who knows how to handle these things."

"Who?" Bryson demanded, stepping closer. "Who did you hire?"

Bugsy stalled. He was clearly terrified of revealing any more information, but he also knew that he had no choice. Antoine still had the gun pointed at him, and the look in his eyes made it clear that he was not afraid to use it.

"I... I can't tell you," Bugsy stammered. "He's... he's dangerous. More dangerous than you. If he finds out I told you..."

"He won't find out," Antoine reasoned. "Unless you tell him. Now, who did you hire?"

Bugsy swallowed hard, his throat bobbing nervously. He knew he was walking a tightrope, balancing between Antoine and the man he was about to name. He took a deep breath, then blurted out the name.

"It was... it was Silas. Silas 'The Ghost'."

A chill ran down Antoine and Bryson's spines. Silas "The Ghost" was a legend in the criminal underworld.

He was rumored to be responsible for dozens of unsolved murders. He was known for his ruthlessness, his efficiency, and his ability to disappear without a trace.

"Silas?" Antoine repeated. "You hired Silas to kill Autumn?"

Bugsy nodded slowly, his body jittery. "He's... he's the best. The most discreet. Sterling said he wanted it done right. Clean. No loose ends."

"And you thought Silas was a good choice?" Bryson asked, his voice dripping with sarcasm. "A guy known for making people disappear?"

"I... I didn't have a choice," Bugsy gulped, his voice pleading. "Sterling gave the order. I just followed it."

The burden of Bugsy's confession settled heavily in the room. They had their answer, but it was far more complicated, far more dangerous, than they had anticipated. They weren't just dealing with a local thug; they were dealing with a powerful university president and a legendary hitman.

"So, Sterling ordered the hit, and Silas carried it out," Antoine said, his voice thoughtful. "And you... you just facilitated it?"

Bugsy nodded miserably.

"Aight," Antoine said, lowering the gun slightly. "That's enough for tonight. You've given us what we came for."

Bugsy let out a shaky breath of relief, but it was short-lived. Antoine raised the gun again, aiming it directly at Bugsy's chest.

"But," Antoine continued, his voice hardening. "If you ever breathe a word of this to anyone, if you so much as look at us funny again, I'll come back. And next time, I won't be asking questions. Got it?"

Bugsy nodded vigorously. "Got it! Got it! I won't say a thing! I swear!"

Antoine held his stare, then slowly lowered the gun. "Good."

"You're letting him go?" Bryson asked, his voice incredulous. "After everything he just told us?"

Antoine shrugged. "He's a fucking small fry. We got what we needed. Sterling and Silas are the ones we need to focus on."

Bryson said nothing, but his jaw was tight. He raised his own gun, aiming it at Bugsy.

"This is for my sister you piece ah shit."

"Bryson, what the hell are you doing!?" Antoine shouted, but it was too late.

Bryson fired. Bugsy stumbled, cried out, and then crashed to the ground. He did not move.

Bryson slowly lowered his gun. "He was a loose end, he knew too much. He woulda snitched. Sterling woulda found us. Plus, the dick-head hired the hit on my sister. Fuck him!"

Antoine held his gun up at the other men.

"And now we don't have to worry about him," Bryson added, his eyes hard.

"Shit," said Antoine. "But from now on don't pull anything like that without talking to me first. Got it?"

Bryson nodded, but there was no regret in his eyes.

He and Bryson backed away, keeping their eyes on Bugsy's men. They moved quickly, making sure no one made any sudden moves. They ran back the way they came. Behind them, footsteps pounded. Voices yelled. More gunshots—wild, panicked shots that hit nothing but walls and ceiling. They slipped out the door and into the night. Trevor had the van running, passenger door open.

"Go, go, go!" Bryson yelled.

They piled in. Trevor gunned it before Antoine even got his door closed. The van fishtailed, tires screaming, then caught traction. They rocketed toward the gate.

The guard stepped out of his booth, hand on his holster. Trevor aimed straight for him. The guard dove aside at the last second. The van clipped the closing gate, metal shrieking against metal, then they were through.

Behind them, headlights flared to life. The SUV. Giving chase.

"Faster!" Antoine yelled.

"I'm going as fast as it goes!" Trevor took a corner too fast, the van tilting dangerously.

Bryson looked back. The SUV was gaining, its engine roaring. A head leaned out the passenger window. Gun in hand.

"Get down!"

The rear window exploded. Safety glass showered the interior. Another shot punched through the van's side panel.

Trevor jerked the wheel, cutting through a gas station parking lot. The SUV followed, its tires smoking. They emerged onto a main road, traffic light and sparse at this hour. Trevor ran a red light, horns blaring. The SUV ran it too.

"Take the next right," Antoine commanded. "Then left. Then right again."

Trevor obeyed. They twisted through residential streets, the van's suspension protesting every turn. Bryson watched the headlights behind them. Still there. Still coming.

Then they weren't. The SUV had fallen back, disappeared around a corner. Trevor kept driving, didn't slow down for another five minutes. Finally, on a dark side street, he pulled over. Killed the lights.

They sat in silence, breathing hard, listening for engine sounds. Nothing but crickets.

"What happened in there?" Trevor probed.

"We got what we needed," Antoine said grimly. "Let's go!"

Trevor started the van again. "Where to?"

"Somewhere safe," Antoine said. "Then we plan. Because next time, we're not running away. Next time, we're finishing this."

Antoine looked at Bryson. "Silas 'The Ghost'," he recalled, shaking his head. "Who would have thought?"

"This shit wild," Bryson added.

Trevor put the van into gear, and they pulled off.

Chapter 29- Sage & Mrs. Hayes

The morning light seeped through the gauzy kitchen curtains, painting the linoleum floor in faded yellow squares. The air was smothered with the rich, savory scent of onions and peppers sautéing in oil—a smell that was warm, like a comforting blanket. Mrs. Hayes moved about the kitchen, her movements confident. She hummed a soft, old-world tune, the melody tinged with a wistful nostalgia that filled the small space.

Sage sat at the kitchen table. She stared out the window at the sleepy street. A haze of heat shimmered above the asphalt, blurring the edges of the houses across the way. She felt strangely calm, a sense of temporary peace settling over her like the morning's humidity. Last night's frantic energy, the tension of Antoine's trailer and the sheer danger of their plan seemed miles away.

Here, in Mrs. Hayes' kitchen, there was only warmth and the soothing aroma of cooking.

"Did you sleep well, mija?" Mrs. Hayes asked, her voice soft as she turned from the stove.

Sage managed a small smile. "Yes ma'am. Actually better than I thought I would." Then she laughed, a short, self-deprecating sound. "Though when I went to the bathroom this morning... I barely recognized myself. My face is still a mess." She touched the area where her eye was still healing. Swollen, black and red due to busted blood vessels.

Mrs. Hayes's eyes grew tender. "Oh, mija. It will heal. Time heals all wounds, as they say." She stirred the ingredients in the pan, the rhythmic clinking of the spoon against the metal a comforting sound.

"Here. This will make you feel better, Autumn's favorite breakfast. Mangú."

She set a plate down in front of Sage—a mound of creamy mashed plantains topped with bright red onions cooked in vinegar. The aroma was intoxicating, rich and earthy. Sage's stomach grumbled despite her nerves. She took a bite, the flavors exploding in her mouth. It was surprisingly hearty, the tang of the onions cutting through the sweetness of the plantains.

"This is amazing," Sage gushed, her eyes widening. "I've never had anything like it."

Mrs. Hayes smiled, a genuine, warm smile that lit up her face. "It's Dominican food. My country's national breakfast. Autumn loved it. She would wake up every morning and ask for plátano con cebolla. It's plantain with onions. She could eat it every day."

"I can see why," Sage beamed, taking another bite. "It's so... so good."

Just then, Gabriel wandered into the kitchen, rubbing his eyes sleepily. He was still in his pajamas, his hair sticking up in unruly tufts. He looked at Sage with innocent eyes.

"Sage," he said softly.

"Hey, Gabriel," Sage replied, returning his gentle gaze. Her heart softened at the sight of the little boy. "Did you sleep well?"

Gabriel nodded. "Abuela made mangú?" he asked, pointing at Sage's plate.

"I did," Mrs. Hayes said, scooping a generous portion onto another plate. "And there is plenty for you too, mi chico."

Gabriel's face lit up, and he scrambled into a chair, his small legs swinging beneath it. As he dug into his breakfast, the kitchen filled with the sounds of munching. Mrs. Hayes watched them both with a soft expression, a hint of sadness mixed with the warmth in her eyes.

"Autumn loved having you here, Sage," Mrs. Hayes said quietly, her voice laced with emotion. "You were like a part of the family. Like the sister she never had. My other daughter."

Sage's throat tightened. "She was like family to me too, Mrs. Hayes. More like family than... well, than my own family."

Mrs. Hayes reached out and took Sage's hand, her touch firm and comforting. "I know, mija. I know your parents are not always around. But you always have a place here. Always. You're my daughter now, whether you like it or not."

Sage's eyes welled up with tears, and she squeezed Mrs. Hayes' hand. "Thank you," she whispered. "Thank you for everything."

The only sound was the soft clinking of forks on plates and Gabriel's happy murmurs as he devoured his mangú. A quiet moment, a brief break from the turmoil that surrounded them. But beneath the surface of the peaceful scene, the unspoken weight of their shared grief was still present.

"She had such a big heart, Autumn," Mrs. Hayes said, her voice a little shaky. "Always looking out for others. Always wanting to make sure everyone was okay."

Sage nodded, wiping away a tear that had escaped. "She did. She cared so much. Sometimes, I think she cared too much."

"She would have done anything for her friends," Mrs. Hayes said with a sad smile. "Like you, mija. You were always there for her, too. You two were inseparable."

"I wish I could have done more," Sage murmured, her voice packed with guilt. "I wish I could have protected her."

Mrs. Hayes shook her head gently. "Don't say that mija. You did everythin' you could. You were a good friend to my Autumn. The best. Don't ever doubt that."

"I wish I had a mom like you," Sage blurted out suddenly, the words tumbling out before she could stop them. She covered her mouth. "I didn't mean that. I mean, you a good mom. And I have a mom, it's just I ain't that close with her or my dad. I'm only close with Antoine."

Mrs. Hayes reached out to stroke Sage's hair. "Oh, mija," she said gently. "You don't have to explain. I understand. Family is... complicated sometimes. But it doesn't mean you don't deserve love, or... a place to belong."

Sage leaned into Mrs. Hayes' touch. She had never felt this sense of unconditional acceptance, this feeling of being truly cared for. It was foreign.

"You can come here whenever you need to. You are always welcome," Mrs. Hayes said softly, her voice filled with genuine affection.

Tears streamed down Sage's face now, and she didn't try to stop them. She let herself cry, letting out the grief and the loneliness she had been holding inside for so long.

Gabriel, sensing the shift in mood, climbed out of his chair and came to stand beside Sage. He patted her hand awkwardly. "Don't cry, Sage," he said softly.

Sage wiped away her tears and gave him a watery smile. "I'm okay, Gabriel," she said, her voice a little shaky. "Just... just a little sad."

He looked at her for a bit, then pointed at her mangú. "More mangú?" he offered.

Sage laughed, a real laugh this time, despite the tears still clinging to her lashes. "Sure, Gabriel. More plátanos sounds perfect."

Mrs. Hayes smiled, her eyes shining with understanding. She refilled Sage's plate, the warmth of the food mirroring the warmth in her heart. The sun had broken out and shone bright. The kitchen was now bathed in a warm, golden glow. Gabriel had moved on to coloring at the table, meticulously filling in a page with vibrant blues and greens. Mrs. Hayes cleared the empty plates.

Sage looked at the scene before her, this quiet slice of domesticity, and a pang of longing struck her. She thought of her own home, the distant coolness between her parents. She realized that what she craved, what Autumn had always found here, was a sense of belonging, a place where she could simply be.

"You know," Mrs. Hayes said, "Autumn always worried about you, mija. About you being alone."

Sage looked up, surprised. "Alone?"

"She knew you didn't always feel... understood. By your family, I mean," Mrs. Hayes clarified gently. "She wanted to make sure you were okay. That you had someone to count on. She always said you were strong, so strong, but even the strongest need to know they are cared for. She wanted you to know that you were never truly alone. That you have her always with you."

Sage's throat tightened again. She hadn't realized how much Autumn had worried; how much she had seen. She had always assumed that Autumn, with her bright personality and seemingly easygoing nature, had everything figured out. But now, looking back, she saw the depth of Autumn's empathy, the quiet observation that had allowed her to see beneath the surface.

"She was right," Sage whispered, looking over at Gabriel, who was now humming happily as he colored. "I did feel alone. A lot of the time."

"But you don't have to anymore," Mrs. Hayes said, placing a warm hand on Sage's arm. "You have us now. Gabriel, me... even Bryson, in his own way. We're your family now, mija. And families, they stick together. They look out for each other. Through thick and thin."

Sage nodded, a sense of gratitude filling her. She looked around the sunny kitchen, at the cheerful clutter, at the warm, loving faces. She wasn't alone. She had people who cared about her, people who would stand by her side, no matter what.

Gabriel looked up from his coloring page. He held up his drawing, a riot of blues and greens that somehow conveyed a sense of joyful chaos. "Look-it, Sage! A monster."

Sage smiled, a smile that reached her eyes. She took the drawing and examined it closely. It looked like a swamp.

"He's a very colorful monster, Gabriel," she said. "I think he's a scary monster."

Gabriel beamed. "He is!"

Sage was grateful for the time to heal, for the warm meals, for Gabriel's colorful drawings, and for Mrs.

Hayes' unwavering love. She was grateful for this sanctuary, this safe harbor in the storm.

225

Chapter 30- Trevor, Bryson & Antoine

The sun rays reached through the van and tapped on Bryson's eyelids. His muscles were aching. He smelled the scent of gun smoke clinging to his clothes.

Antoine's face was set like granite. He stared straight ahead, the events of the night playing out in his head. Trevor in the back snored softly, oblivious to the growing light. They had slept rough, but they had survived.

"Man, I feel like I wrestled a grizzly bear all night," Bryson reminisced, rubbing his eyes.

Antoine chuckled, his voice still rough with sleep. "You look like you did." He ran a hand through his hair, trying to tame the unruly strands. "Let's get outta this tin can. I feel like a sardine."

They climbed out from the van, stretching and groaning in the cool morning air. The delivery van was parked off a desolate road, hidden behind a screen of overgrown shrubs. The location had served its purpose for the night, but now they needed to get moving.

"Where's your truck?" Trevor asked, finally emerging from his slumber. He rubbed his eyes and looked around in confusion.

"Hidden nearby. We ditched it over there last night." Antoine went over to a brush, then he jumped into his truck. He hopped out of his truck and went back over to the men.

"I need to return this," Antoine said, referring to the van. Bryson nodded, still feeling the rawness of the previous night's actions. "Right. And then what?"

"Then we regroup," Antoine replied. "Figure out where we stand."

Just then, Bryson's phone buzzed. He pulled it out, seeing his mom's name flash across the screen. He answered.

Yeah?" he mumbled, still half-asleep.

"Brysonito? Is that you?" Mrs. Hayes's voice was filled with concern.

"Yeah, it's me mama. Is everything alright?" Bryson asked.

"Yes, I was just worried. You didn't come by this morning. I made mangu," she said.

"We... we good, mama. We had to get moving early. We slept in the van last night," Bryson explained, trying to sound reassuring.

"In the van? Oh, mijo... Are you safe?"

"Yeah we good mama. Don't worry. We just grabbing some breakfast now," he said, hoping to ease her mind.

"And Sage? Is she doing any better?" he inquired.

"She's doing alright. She even had some mangu. She loved it," said Mrs. Hayes.

"God bless your mom for taking care of my sister," interjected Antoine.

Bryson relayed the message to his mother.

"I just want to make sure you and your friend are okay. You both come by when you have a moment," Mrs. Hayes added.

"We will, mama. I promise. We'll see you later. I gotta go now," he said, eager to get moving.

"Okay, mijo. God bless you. Be careful," she said.

"We will. Love ya, mama," Bryson replied, and ended the call.

Antoine got back into the delivery van. "Follow me," he commanded. Bryson followed behind in the pickup truck. Antoine drove to a less traveled section of town, parking behind a small garage. A man emerged, his eyes wary as he approached the delivery van.

"Antoine, you back," he said with a questioning look. "Everything alright?"

"Yeah, all set," Antoine said curtly. He slid out of the van.

"What did you need it for?" the man asked.

"Business. What do you need to know for?" Antoine stated coldly. The man shrugged, his expression uneasy. "Just curious, tough guy. Just, uh, glad to have it back."

He turned and began to inspect the van.

"What the fuck happend to my van?"

Before he could complain about the damages Antoine dashed into the pickup, and they were off. As they drove away, Trevor finally spoke.

"I... I stink. We all do. We need a shower."

Antoine snorted. "There's no shower until we handle our business, Trev."

"We need to clean up at some point. Can't keep walking around smelling like we crawled out of a dumpster," responded Trevor. "Just focus on what we must do," Bryson said, his voice firm. "We're so close."

A few minutes later, Antoine pulled into the parking lot of a Dunkin' Donuts. "Breakfast," he announced. "We need some dang fuel."

They went inside and grabbed bagels and coffee, finding a booth in the corner. They ate without saying a word for a few minutes, the weariness settling heavily upon them. Trevor spoke. "So, where do we go from here?"

"We pay President Sterling a little visit," Bryson said, taking a bite of his bagel.

"He lives in a house next to the university," Trevor revealed.

"Then it's time for a house call," Antoine said. "We pay him a visit at his home. Morning time. Catch him off guard."

Chapter 31- Trevor, Bryson, Antoine & President Sterling

After breakfast, they drove to Sterling's house. It was set back from the street with manicured lawns and a wrought-iron fence. They tried the front gate, but it was locked.

"Well, this is just great," Bryson observed. "Looks like we're not getting in."

"I know a trick," Trevor said. "Follow me."

Antoine parked his pickup truck in the alumni parking lot. Trevor brought them to a gate at the side of the building that led way to a pathway of flowers resembling a mini botanical garden. At the end of the pathway was the president's house. Trevor explained how he'd learn about the pathway and that they had forgotten to close the gate because no one knew about it.

They walked up to the house and rang the doorbell. A few moments later, the door was opened by a man. He was a white man, probably in his late fifties, with thinning gray hair and a nervous demeanor. He had a smattering of white powder just below his nose that he frantically tried to brush away when he saw the three men.

"Yes? What do you want?" Sterling asked.

Before he could react, Antoine and Bryson pushed their way into the house. Antoine shoved Sterling against the wall, pistol whipping him. Sterling cried out, fear and confusion etched on his face.

A woman came running from another room. "What's going on? Who are you?"

Bryson moved quickly, grabbing her arm.

"Don't scream. Just stay quiet, and no one will get hurt." He grabbed the rope Trevor brought and tied her hands.

"What do you want? Money? I'll give you whatever you want. Just don't hurt us," begged Sterling.

"We don't want your money," Antoine said. "We want answers."

"Answers? A...About what?" Sterling stammered.

"About Autumn Hayes," Bryson said, his eyes burning into Sterling's.

Sterling's face paled even further. "Hayes? I... I don't know any Autumn Hayes."

"Don't lie to us," Bryson exploded, his grip tightening on the woman's arm. "She was my sister."

Sterling's eyes widened in shock. "Your sister? Oh my god."

"Yeah, my sister. And you're the reason she's dead," Bryson said. "You and your little drug ring."

Sterling's wife looked at her husband in disbelief. "Drugs? What is he talking about, Richard?"

"You didn't know?" Bryson confessed to the woman. "That your husband is a drug kingpin? That he uses the university for his operation?"

President Sterling's wife gasped. "That's not true! Richard, tell me it's not true!"

"Betsy don't listen to him," said Sterling.

"It's true, Betsy," Bryson said. "Your husband is a monster. He had my sister killed because she found out what he was doing. She was going to expose him, and he couldn't let that happen."

"That's not... that's not how it was," Sterling stammered, his eyes darting nervously between the three men.

"Then tell us how it was," Antoine said. "Tell us everything, or you'll wish you never met Autumn

Hayes." He pistol whipped him again and blood trickled down his forehead.

"I... I didn't want her dead," Sterling pleaded, tears running down his face. "I just... I just wanted her to stay quiet. She knew too much. I told her to back off. I told her to mind her business, but she wouldn't listen."

"So, you had her killed?" Bryson said, his voice flat.

"No! I didn't... I didn't order it, not directly. I just... I just told my people to... to take care of the problem. I didn't mean for them to... to kill her."

"Take care of the problem? What the fuck does that mean?" Bryson asked, his body trembling with rage.

"It means... it means making sure she didn't talk. It means scaring her, intimidating her. That's all I wanted. I swear."

"But they killed her anyway," Bryson said, his voice hollow.

"Yes," Sterling sobbed. "Yes, they did. I didn't want that. I swear I didn't. You don't understand... I was cornered! I never signed her death warrant, I swear it."

Bryson shook his head in disgust. "You're a liar, Sterling. And a coward." He looked at Antoine, who shook his head.

Trevor stood near the entrance, watching the scene unfold. He looked out the front window, making sure no one was coming. He was also trying to make sense of everything he was hearing. He never knew president Sterling to be this way. He was always a nice man in his interactions.

Suddenly, Bryson snatched Sterling by the collar and shoved him against the wall.

"Fuck boy you took my sister from me," he said, his voice shaking. "You took her life, and I'll never forgive you for that." He drew his handgun.

Sterling's wife began to scream, a high-pitched, piercing sound that filled the room.

"No! Richard! Please, don't!"

Bryson's hand wavered for a fraction of a second, but he had his mind made up. "Any last words, Mr. President?" he asked, his voice devoid of emotion.

Sterling's eyes shifted between Bryson and Antoine, pleading. "Just... just don't kill my wife. I love you, Betsy."

Betsy continued screaming. It was like she was watching a nightmare unfold, and she was unable to wake from it. She never imagined her husband to be a man like this, to be capable of so much. He had been lying to her for years.

Bryson's finger tightened on the trigger. The sound of the gunshot was deafening in the confined space, a sharp crack that seemed to echo in their ears. Blood splattered across Betsy's face, hot and wet. President

Sterling's body slumped to the floor, his eyes still open, staring blankly at the ceiling.

Betsy's screams turned into choked sobs, her body shaking violently. "Richard! Oh god, Richard!"

"Be quiet!" Antoine snapped, his voice harsh. "Or you'll be next."

Betsy's sobs quieted. She stared at her husband's lifeless body, her mind struggling to process what had just happened. Life had been extinguished from his body as quickly as flipping a light switch. All that remained was a bloody mess and her screams.

Bryson looked at her, his face impassive. "He had to die. He killed Autumn. He thought he could get away with it. Nah. Never."

Betsy shook her head in disbelief. "No... no, he wouldn't... he couldn't..." Her voice trailed off, unable to fully grasp the reality of the situation.

Antoine glanced at Bryson, a silent communication passing between them. He raised his gun and put a bullet through Betsy's forehead. Her body dropped right next to her husband's.

It was time to go. They had done what they came to do.

"Let's go," Antoine said.

They slipped back out through the botanical garden pathway, the same way they had come in. The morning was still young, but the events inside the house felt like they had happened in another lifetime.

As they made their way back to Antoine's pickup truck, Bryson spoke. "Someone will find 'em soon."

"Who gives a shit," Antoine replied.

They drove in silence for a few minutes, the weight of what they had done pressing down on them. The adrenaline that had been coursing through their veins began to fade, replaced by bone-deep weariness.

"One more," Bryson said.

"Silas," Antoine mouthed.

Trevor, who had been silent the entire time, finally spoke up, his voice quiet. "Silas... he's not going to be easy to find. He's... he's like his name. A ghost. He comes and goes, and no one ever really knows where he is."

"We'll find him," Bryson avowed. "We must. He's the one who took Autumn away from me. He's the one who needs to pay the most."

The weight of the next task settled upon them. They had taken down Sterling, a significant player, but the true mastermind, the one who had orchestrated it all, was still out there. Silas "The Ghost." They had taken down the head of the snake but not the whole snake itself. He was the one they were hunting for now. Antoine gripped the steering wheel. He knew this was going to be the hardest part, the most dangerous part, but he was ready. They had come this far; they had sacrificed too much to turn back now. They would find Silas and they would make him pay for what he had done. A promise, a vow, etched in blood and grief.

Chapter 32- Silas

The scent of jasmine, a sweet, almost cloying fragrance filled the expansive foyer. Sunlight streamed through the stained-glass windows, painting intricate patterns on the polished marble floor. This wasn't the place one would associate with a ghost, not a ghost of violence. This was a home of comfort, of laughter, a sanctuary of a different kind. A sanctuary he had built for his grandmother.

She called him Riley, a soft name, unlike the sharp, angular alias he wore like armor. Riley was the boy who brought her tea in delicate China mugs, the grandson who meticulously tended her rose garden, the man who ensured she had every thing her heart desired. Silas, on the other hand, was a demon, a whisper in the dark, a name spoken only in hushed tones by those who needed a problem... permanently solved.

He sat at the sprawling oak kitchen table, the morning newspaper spread before him, but his eyes scanned the lines without truly seeing them. The headline glared back at him: *University's President Found Dead.* He scoffed. Sterling had never had the spine to survive. Then there was another article, a brief mention of local gang leaders found dead in separate incidents. "Junior," he muttered, "and Bugsy." They were sloppy, but they were useful for a time. It was always the sloppy ones who dragged him into the light.

He swirled the dark coffee in his mug, watching the ripples dissipate. He knew what this meant. $200,000. That's what they'd paid him to murder Autumn. A hefty sum, but it was just another job. There was no malice, no personal vendetta. Just business. He'd done what he was asked. Dropped her body in the murky swamp, the gators a convenient and efficient disposal system. He'd felt nothing. He rarely did.

But this... this felt different. These deaths, so close together, so messy, so... personal, indicated that someone was poking around. Someone who knew too much. Someone who was coming for him.

A small, warm hand rested on his shoulder.

"Riley, dear, you're frowning again. Is something troubling you?"

He looked up. He met his grandmother's kind, wrinkled face. Her bright blue eyes, wise from a lifetime of trials, met his with unwavering love. Though small and fragile-looking, her spirit burned indomitable. She wore a flowered dress that billowed around her like a summer cloud, her white hair neatly pulled back in a bun. This was his lifeline, the only tether he had to a world that wasn't painted in shades of blood and death.

"Just... business, Grandma," he said, forcing a smile. "Lots of moving parts."

She patted his hand. "Business is always complicated, isn't it? But you're a smart boy, Riley. You'll figure it out." She poured herself a cup of tea, the delicate floral scent mingling with the rich aroma of her grandson's coffee.

"This house... it's beautiful, Grandma," Silas said, as he looked over the spacious kitchen. The custom cabinetry, the gleaming granite countertops, the hand-painted tiles—he'd spared no expense. He'd personally overseen every detail, every intricate design, ensuring it was perfect for her. "I'm glad you like it."

Her eyes twinkled. "Like it? I love it! It's more than I ever dreamed of. You've given me a palace, Riley. My sweet, generous boy."

He chuckled softly. She had no idea where the money came from, and he intended to keep it that way.

All she knew was that Riley took care of her, that he provided for her in ways she never thought possible. She saw only the devoted grandson, the doting caregiver. She couldn't, wouldn't, see the hitman that lurked beneath.

"I remember when this was just a patch of overgrown weeds," she reminisced, sipping her tea. "We lived in that tiny, drafty house in Michigan. Remember how cold it used to get in the winter?"

He remembered all too well. He remembered huddling under thin blankets, his stomach always rumbling, the sound of his parents' arguments echoing through the walls. He remembered the night they didn't come home. He'd been just a boy, barely old enough to understand. They'd been murdered, their lives snuffed out in a senseless act of violence. He'd been left alone, crying in the dark, until his grandmother came and held him, her soft voice whispering promises that she would always protect him.

His parents' deaths had shaped him. The bitterness had taken root, poisoning his soul, turning him into something hard. He learned that the world was a cruel place, that people could be bought and sold, that violence was the ultimate currency. He learned how to be useful, how to make himself invaluable to those who needed a problem removed. He became Silas "The Ghost."

"You took me in," he said, his voice rough with emotion. "When no one else would. You gave me a home, a life. I owe you everything."

"Nonsense," she said, patting his hand again. "You're family, Riley. I'd do anything for you." She looked at him with those bright blue eyes, penetrating, almost unsettling. "Are you sure everything is alright, dear? You seem... distant."

He stood up, needing to move, to put some space between himself and her unwavering gaze. "I just have a lot on my mind."

"Are you in trouble, Riley? Is there something you're not telling me?"

He forced a reassuring smile. "No, Grandma. Nothing like that. Just... complicated."

"Okay, cause you got me worried," she responded.

"Grandma, you worry too much."

He went to the large window that overlooked the meticulously landscaped backyard. He'd built this oasis for her, a paradise of roses and sculpted hedges and trickling fountains. He watched a hummingbird hover near a vibrant hibiscus, its wings a blur of motion. Such fragile, beautiful creatures, so easily broken.

He thought of Autumn. He'd done his research, as he always did. He'd learned about her, her life, her friends, her connections. He'd seen the photos, the smiling face, the bright eyes full of hope. It was always easier when they were just names, just targets. But sometimes... sometimes, the faces stayed with him.

He'd seen the name Bryson Hayes when he had looked up Autumn. A connection, a brother, a threat.

He retrieved his black duffel bag from behind a closet in his bedroom. It revealed an insignia of a bobcat's claw at the front. He'd fallen in love with bobcats when he was little. The first and only time he saw one was in the swamp at night. He was eleven. He thought of himself as a bobcat, stealthy and hard to catch. So much that he wore boots with claws indented in the soles. The boots left bobcat prints on the ground when he walked. He put the claw symbol on everything, even his victims.

He opened his duffel bag. His weapons needed to be cleaned. He knew Bryson could be trouble, and he was going to get rid of him. The only way to deal with a problem is head on. He didn't want a full war but if one came his way he would be ready.

Silas slipped out to his Ram 1500, parked discreetly in the garage. He'd spent hours modifying it, installing hidden compartments, and reinforcing the frame. It was his mobile arsenal, his escape vehicle, his silent partner. Behind his grandma's back, he loaded his duffel bag, heavy with guns, knives, and other... tools of his trade.

As always, he made a mental note of the contents, checking to make sure everything was in its place.

Returning inside, he found his grandmother humming softly as she arranged a bouquet of freshly cut roses. She was so content, so blissfully unaware of the darkness he carried within him.

"Grandma," he called, his voice gentle, "I need to go away for a few days. Seeing a friend."

She turned, her eyes full of concern. "Oh, Riley, must you? I was hoping we could spend some more time together."

"I'll be back soon," he promised. "And when I come back, we'll have a big dinner. Your favorite. And we'll watch movies all night long."

She smiled, accepting his assurance. "Alright, dear. But be careful. And call me, won't you? Let me know you're alright."

"Of course, Grandma," he reassured, giving her a hug.

He left soon after, the image of her kind face etched in his mind. As he drove, the jasmine scent faded, replaced by the smell of leather and gun oil that permeated the truck's interior. He pulled onto the interstate, the hum of the tires a steady drone.

Chapter 33- Trevor, Bryson & Antoine

The ride back was a funeral march played out on blacktop. Bryson stared out the window, but he wasn't seeing much except Silas dancing in his head. Trevor, sat rigid as a board in the back, like any sudden move might shatter him to pieces.

The midday sun blazed down.

Antoine's voice finally cut through the air as they pulled up to Mrs. Hayes's place. "So," he drawled. "Anything at all?"

Bryson shook his head; weariness etched deep in the lines around his eyes. "Nothing. It's like trying to nail down smoke." He rubbed his temples, a gesture against the headache that hammered at him. "We don't even know if that's his real name."

Trevor piped up from the back. "We don't know what he looks like either. I hear whispers, but nothing solid. He could be any old Joe Blow. Passing us by on the street and we wouldn't know a thing." He gestured vaguely at the houses along the street. "Could be our neighbor for all we know."

Antoine stared out at the sun-bleached lawns.

"He could be hiding in plain sight. Blending in like a chameleon on a porch swing. We wouldn't know him from a can of paint." He glanced at Bryson. "If you ain't... well, maybe if Bugsy was still breathin', he mighta coughed up a name, a face. Something."

Bryson's eyes flashed, a dark fire sparked behind them. "It was him or us, Antoine. You saw it. Don't start with the ifs and maybes."

Antoine let out a long, slow breath.

"I ain't sayin' nothin', just thinking out loud. We heard stories 'bout this fuck-face, bad stories, things that crawl under your skin. Yet no one knows what this ass-wipe looks like."

Silence stretched, broken only by the hum of the idling engine. Then Antoine sighed, the fight drained out of him.

"Look, we're chasing our tails here. We got no nothin'. Is there any way we ever find this Silas, any way at all?" he looked from Bryson to Trevor, searchin' for an answer in their eyes. "Maybe we oughta just split up, go our own ways."

Trevor's eyes widened, fear flashing in their depths. "What? No way! We can't quit now. Autumn wouldn't want us to quit."

Antoine shrugged, a weary slump on his shoulders. "How the fuck we gon' find Silas? Besides, detectives been blowing up Bryson's phone. Shit gettin' hot. Too hot."

Bryson nodded. "He's right. We can't keep rolling together like this. It's like we put a target on backs." He pulled out his phone and stared at the screen. "This is how they find you. By making yourself easy to find."

They decided to drop Trevor off first. His apartment was just a few blocks from the university, a short distance, but it felt like crossing a minefield. Every silhouette seemed to hold a threat, every passing car a potential enemy.

"Be careful," Bryson told Trevor as he climbed out of the truck. "Keep your head down. And text us as soon as you get inside."

Trevor nodded, a shiver running through him. He looked back before turning away, "If anything happens to me," Trevor's voice hitched, his gaze locking with both of theirs, "Make sure y'all handle it."

As they drove off, Antoine turned to Bryson. "We gotta talk to Sage and Mrs. Hayes. Keep it short, keep it simple. Just tell 'em it's handled. Everything's taken care of."

Bryson frowned. "Handled how? What we gonna say? That we closer? We ain't closer, we just more confused!"

Antoine flicked him with a sharp look.

"Just say it's taken care of, dang. We don't need to drown them with our troubles, Bryson. Give 'em peace, or something close to it. Can you at least do that?"

They pulled up to Mrs. Hayes's house. Antoine sighed. "I need to head back to the trailer. Gonna take Sage with me. Need to get away from all this and think things out," he rubbed his tired eyes.

Inside, Mrs. Hayes greeted them with a warm smile but worry still flickered in her eyes. Sage was sittin' on the couch. Gabriel ran over to Bryson and wrapped his arms around his legs.

Bryson went over to Sage, lookin' her over.

"Glad you're doing better, Sage."

Sage smiled faintly and reached for his hand. Their fingers intertwined, a brief but powerful connection that spoke volumes of their shared experiences. In that moment, there was an intimacy between them, a silent understanding that no one else could fully grasp.

Bryson noticed something in her eyes.

"What's wrong, Sage?" he asked softly.

Sage glanced around the room before leaning close. "Just... scared. Scared it'll never end. Scared we won't find who did this to Autumn."

Bryson squeezed her hand. "I'm not gonna let anyone hurt you, Sage. I promise. And we won't quit until we find out who did it. I swear."

Bryson stood and went over to Mrs. Hayes. He embraced her, a warm, wordless connection passing between them. "Mama, I gotta head home soon. Got work in the morning at the hospital," said Bryson.

"Of course, Brysonito," Mrs. Hayes replied, patting his hand. "You do what you need to do mijo."

The house was still, the only sound the rhythmic tick-tock of the grandfather clock in the corner. Every tick felt like a missed opportunity, a moment lost, a chance of finding Silas that slipped further away.

Bryson stirred, the weight of his unspoken thoughts dense on his chest. "Antoine," he began, "You think we doin' the right thing? Just... lettin' things lie for a bit?"

Antoine, who had been staring out the window, turned slowly. His eyes, usually filled with a fiery intensity, held exhaustion.

"What's right ain't always what's easy, Bryson. And what's easy ain't always what's smart. We rush out there half-cocked, we just paint bigger targets on our backs. Remember? We gotta be smarter than them, not louder."

"But time ain't on our side," Bryson countered. "Silas... whoever he is, he's got a head start. And he ain't sittin' still, that's for fuckin' sure."

Antoine walked over to the table, his movements slow, deliberate. "We split up," he said. "Like we talked about. But... we ain't just going our separate ways. We each take a piece of the puzzle. You keep digging into what Trevor said. See if there's anything connected to this Silas. I'll... I'll try to shake some trees, see what I can rattle loose from my old contacts. And Trevor, well..." he trailed off.

"Trevor needs to lie low," Bryson finished. "Somewhere safe. Until we figure this out."

"Exactly," Antoine agreed. "But first..." He turned to Bryson. "First, we gotta deal with the cops. They're callin' you, right? Blowin' up your phone?"

Bryson nodded, pulling his phone from his pocket. It buzzed again, Detective Mason's name flashing across the screen. He let it go to voicemail. "Yeah. They want to talk. About Autumn, about... everything."

"Then you talk," Antoine suggested, his tone surprisingly calm. "But don't tell them anything. Give 'em just enough. Lead 'em down a side road, keep 'em busy while we do our own work."

"You think that'll work?" Bryson asked, a note of doubt creeping into his voice. "They're not stupid, Antoine. They'll see right through us."

"Maybe," Antoine shrugged. "But it's better than nothing. Gives us some space to breathe, some time to find Silas before he finds us." He took a gulp of his water, his eyes meeting Bryson's with a hard edge.

"Besides," he added, a hint of steel in his voice, "I think we know a thing or two about deceiving."

Sage, her face bearing the marks of what she'd been through, moved sluggishly, gathering her belongings into a small bag. Antoine watched her with a protective intensity, his hand never far from hers. Mrs. Hayes stood in the doorway. She gave them both a hug.

Antoine settled Sage into the passenger seat of his battered truck, his movements gentle and deliberate. With a final nod to Mrs. Hayes and Bryson, he started the truck. They drove off, leaving behind the sanctuary of Mrs. Hayes's home and venturing back into the uncertain world.

***

Later that evening, Bryson finally answered Detective Mason's call. He had made it back to his house. He stepped out onto his porch. He kept his voice low, his words measured, sticking to the script he had agreed upon with Antoine. He told Mason what he wanted him to hear: that he was cooperating, that he was trying to help, but that he was also scared, confused. He painted a picture of grief and uncertainty, carefully omitting any mention of Silas, of Sterling, of the warehouse, of the growing suspicion that Autumn's death was more than just a random act of violence.

He ended the call with a promise to come down to the station the next day, to give a full statement. A calculated move, a way to buy them some more time.

Chapter 34- Bryson & Silas

The digital clock on Bryson's bedside table glowed: 2:47 AM. He'd only managed a few hours of sleep, his mind still racing. He'd made sure the doors and windows were locked, a comfort against the unease that gnawed at him. His house felt like a fragile shell against an unseen predator.

A faint sound, barely perceptible, broke the stillness. A light scratching, like a twig brushing against the glass. Bryson froze, his senses instantly alert. He held his breath, listening intently. Another scratch, followed by a soft thud. It was coming from outside his bedroom window.

His heart leaped into his throat. It couldn't be... could it? Was it just his imagination, his paranoia running wild? He lay still for a moment, trying to convince himself it was nothing, just a stray branch or an animal rustling in the bushes. But the prickling sensation at the back of his neck told him otherwise.

He inched towards the edge of the bed; his eyes fixed on the window. He reached out a hand and carefully parted the blinds just enough to peek outside. The night was dark, illuminated only by the faint glow of the moon struggling through the clouds. He strained his eyes, but saw nothing. No one. Just the outline of the overgrown shrubs beneath the window and the silhouette of his yard stretching into the distance.

He let out a shaky breath, trying to calm his racing heart. Maybe it was just his imagination. Maybe the stress was getting to him. But as he turned away, a tiny pebble pinged against the glass. He jumped, his muscles tensing.

Again, he parted the blinds, his eyes darting back and forth, searching. Still nothing. Just the shadows of the trees rustling. What he didn't see was Silas. He was pressed tightly against the house on the opposite side of the window's view, melding with the brick work of the house, a full-sized body in a perfect freeze. Silas's eyes shone in the darkness. He was about to test the window lock with a thin metal tool when he heard the soft rustle of movement within. He knew, with certainty, that someone was awake inside. And watching.

The slight shifting of the blinds confirmed his suspicions. He remained motionless, a statue. His patience, a weapon as deadly as any blade. He didn't panic. He didn't rush. He simply waited. He had all night. He would be in the house one way or another.

Bryson, after another long scan, decided it had to be his imagination. The house was quiet again. The sounds had stopped. Surely, if someone was out there, they would have made themselves known by now. He let the blinds fall back into place, a thin layer of fabric offering only the illusion of security and tried to slow his racing heart. Just in case, he grabbed his swiss army knife from the drawer and stuffed it into the waist of his pajama shorts. With a sigh, he climbed back into bed, pulling the covers up to his chin. Maybe, just maybe, he could get a few more hours of sleep before the real problems started.

An hour later Silas decided it was time to make a move. He slipped around the side of the house, his movements fluid and precise, like a predator closing in on its prey. He reached the back door, which was dimly lit by a weak porch light. His long fingers delved into the worn leather bag slung across his back, and he pulled out a set of lock picks. He worked at the lock with ease, the tools clicking softly in the night. In seconds, the lock was sprung, and the door swung open with a delicate creak.

Inside, the house was dark and still, the only sound was the gentle hum of the refrigerator. Silas moved like a ghost, his footsteps silent on the wooden floor. He glided through the rooms, checking each one. He moved with purpose. He wasn't simply searching; he was hunting. There was a predatory quality to his movements, an efficiency that spoke of countless hunts and kills.

He found the living room, with its worn furniture and scattered books. The kitchen, with its lingering scent of coffee. He even paused briefly outside the chocolate room, his eyes catching the slightly ajar door, then continued walking towards the hallway that led to Bryson's bedroom. He paused at Bryson's door. Cautiously, carefully, Silas turned the doorknob, inching the door open. The hinges creaked softly, a sound that seemed deafening in the stillness. He froze, listening. There was a stirring from within, a rustle of sheets. He held his breath, every muscle tense. Bryson had been drifting back to sleep when the creak of the door jolted him awake. His eyes snapped open. He instinctively reached for the handgun he kept in the drawer beside his bed, but he was too slow. Silas sprang forward like a coiled spring. He was across the room in an instant. Before Bryson could react, before he could even fully process what was happening, Silas brought the butt of his gun down hard on the side of Bryson's head. A blinding flash of pain and then... nothing. Bryson's world went black.

When Bryson finally regained consciousness, it was to the unsettling sensation of movement. He was lying down, something rough and cold pressing against his cheek. His head throbbed with a dull, persistent ache, and his mouth felt dry and sticky. He tried to move his arms, but they were bound tight, his wrists and ankles secured with what felt like heavy-duty duct tape. Panic began to set in. Where was he? What had happened? He remembered the noises outside his window, the creaking door... and then the darkness. He tried to open his eyes, but his eyelids felt heavy and sluggish. He managed to crack them open a sliver, enough to see that he was lying in the bed of a pickup truck, the wind whipping past him. The sky above was a vast expanse of dark, star-dusted velvet, the moon casting a pale glow over the passing landscape. He was being moved. He was being taken somewhere.

His mind raced, trying to piece together the fragments of memory, trying to make sense of his situation. The bumpy ride of the truck, the swaying motion, it all felt horribly familiar. Too familiar. A realization began to dawn. This... this felt like what they had done to Autumn.

He could feel the swiss army knife he had tucked into his shorts earlier as it pressed up against his skin. He twisted and grinded against the bed of the truck until it unclipped from his waist. His hands were tied behind his back as he laid on the knife. He managed to roll over onto his back. With tiny movements of his fingers he was able to locate and grab the knife. He forced it open. With the knife held by the tip of his fingers he struggled as he rubbed the duct tape against the tip of the blade. He moved his hands in a back and forth motion.

The truck rattled and lurched over uneven ground, joggling Bryson with each bump. He forced himself to breathe slowly, trying to control his rising panic. He decided to play dead, pretending to still be unconscious. It was the only way to buy some time, to observe his captor without revealing that he was awake. He closed his eyes again, slackening his muscles, letting his body go limp. The ride seemed to go on forever, the monotonous sound of the engine. Each mile took them further away from safety, further into the unknown. He could feel the truck leaving the paved road, the ride becoming rougher, more jarring. The scent of damp earth and decaying vegetation. Finally, the truck slowed to a stop. Leaving only the sounds of the night: the chirping of crickets and the distant hoot of an owl. Bryson held his breath, feigning unconsciousness, his heart pounding in his chest.

He heard the driver door open and close, the sound echoing. Then, footsteps, heavy and deliberate, approaching the back of the truck. He kept his eyes closed, but he could feel the presence of someone standing over him, watching him. He delicately released the swiss army knife from his hands.

The tailgate lowered with a clang, and then strong hands were reaching down, grabbing him. He was lifted, his body slung over a broad shoulder like a sack of potatoes. He managed to keep his body limp. He got a small peak through his slitted eyes. The world was a blur of movement, but he could make out the dense foliage pressing in on either side, the gnarled trunks of trees reaching up like skeletal fingers. This was it. The swamp. Where Autumn had... Where they had taken her.

He squeezed his eyes shut again, trying to control his breathing. He was at the mercy of this man, this ghost, and the thought was paralyzing. He could hear the man's heavy breathing, the rhythmic thud of his boots against the soft earth. He was big. Very big. And strong. Bryson could feel the power radiating from him.

The journey felt like an eternity, each step taking them deeper into the heart of the swamp. The ground beneath them was uneven and spongy, sucking at the man's boots with a wet, sucking sound. Bryson could hear the rustling of unseen creatures in the undergrowth, the croaking of frogs, the distant hoot of an owl. The sounds of the night, usually so comforting, now felt ominous.

Then, they stopped.

Bryson remained still, his body limp, his breathing shallow. He could feel the man's weight shifting, preparing to set him down. He braced himself, trying to anticipate the moment. He was dumped onto the wet, mucky ground. A grunt from Silas signaled that he was finally free from being carried. He tried to maintain the appearance of unconsciousness, even as every muscle in his body screamed for him to move, to fight, to run. He was soaked and cold, every limb felt like lead, he shivered despite his best effort not to. He kept his eyes barely cracked, his vision blurred by the dim moonlight. He noticed a raging wildfire at the corner of his eyes that provided some warmth.

He could see the man now, standing over him like a dark monolith. He was massive, towering over Bryson with an almost inhuman presence. Six feet five inches, maybe more. Broad shoulders, thick arms that looked like they could snap a tree in half. Long, greasy hair hung down to his shoulders, framing a face that was obscured by the night. He was more like a force of nature than a man, a living embodiment of the fear that had haunted Bryson for so long.

Silas reached into his leather bag. Bryson's heart pounded, his mind racing. What was he pulling out? A gun? A knife? Something worse? Every nerve in his body was strung tight, coiled and ready to spring. His legs were tied tightly, his wrists too, his mouth covered with duct tape. He could barely move. He felt completely helpless.

He knew he couldn't stay still any longer. If he was going to have any chance of surviving this, he had to act. He tensed his legs, trying to get some feeling back into them. He tried to roll over, but his bound limbs made it impossible. He managed a slight twitch, a tiny movement that he hoped Silas wouldn't notice.

The movement was just enough.

Silas stopped what he was doing, his head tilting slightly as if he had heard something. He looked down at Bryson.. Bryson froze again, pretending to be completely still. He could feel Silas' gaze on him. Silas reached into his bag and pulled something out. At first, Bryson couldn't make out what it was. But as the man turned it towards the moonlight. It was a branding iron. A heavy metal rod with a twisted, jagged end. He dipped the rod into the wildfire. It glowed a faint red at the tip. It was hot. Burning hot. Bryson's blood ran cold. He knew what was coming. He had heard stories, whispers in the dark corners of the prison yard, about men who used branding irons. A tool of torture. A way to leave a permanent mark, a scar that went deeper than the skin. He could smell the burnt wood from the fire. Silas knelt beside him; the branding iron held loosely in his hand. He looked down at Bryson, a cruel smile playing on his lips. Then, in a voice that was surprisingly soft, he said, "Wakey, wakey, sleepyhead." Bryson's eyes snapped open. The sudden movement was involuntary. He was paralyzed by fear and shock. His eyes locked with Silas's.

Silas chuckled. "I knew you were awake," he said. "You're not as good an actor as you think. Tag, you're it," Silas raised the branding iron. The red-hot tip hissed as it made contact with Bryson's skin. The pain was instantaneous, searing, unbearable. It felt like a white-hot poker was being driven into his flesh. Bryson screamed. The sound was muffled by the duct tape, but it was still a raw, primal cry of agony. His body convulsed, his muscles contracting uncontrollably. He tried to pull away, but he was bound too tightly. He could only writhe on the ground. Silas let out a devilish chuckle, a sound that sent a chill to Bryson's bones. He watched, his eyes filled with a dark amusement, as Bryson thrashed in pain. The smell of burning flesh filled the air. The stench made Bryson feel like he would vomit. In the midst of his agony, Bryson noticed the duct tape around his wrist lost tension. The swiss knife had cut slits into the tape. A tiny sliver of hope ignited in his heart. It was the only thing that kept him going, that kept him from giving up completely.

Silas reached into his bag for something else. That was his chance. Bryson, with every ounce of strength he could muster, began to work at the weakened tape. He pulled and twisted, ignoring the throbbing pain in his branded skin, focusing only on the tiny shred of freedom that was within his reach. He was losing consciousness; the pain was too much. But he had to do this now.

Finally, the tape gave way. His hands were free. He quickly ripped the tape from his feet. Silas turned around. He seemed to sense something had changed. But he was too late. Bryson scrambled to his feet, his legs unsteady, his head spinning. He snatched the branding iron off the ground, the metal still hot in his hand. He faced Silas. Silas was surprised. He hadn't expected this. He took a step back, his hand instinctively going to the gun in his waistband. Bryson didn't hesitate. Bryson swung the iron with desperate fury, cracking Silas's skull with a sickening thud.

Silas roared.

He stumbled back, his massive frame swaying precariously. He fell to his knees; his hands pressed against his head. He was bleeding. A lot. Bryson didn't stop. He kept swinging, fueled by rage and pain and the desperate need to survive. He beat the man with the metal iron rod. Again and again; each blow a release of the agony he had suffered. He screamed at him with every blow. This was for Autumn. This was for Gabriel. This was for every moment of fear, every second of helplessness. Bryson ripped the duct tape from his mouth.

"This is for my sister fuck boy," he yelled, his voice rose to a crescendo. He kept beating Silas until the man finally stopped moving, a lifeless heap on the ground. The metallic scent of blood was everywhere, the wet ground slick beneath his feet. Bryson dropped the branding iron, his chest heaving, his body trembling. He stared down at Silas. It seemed like an out of body experience.

He backed away, stumbled, then fell to the ground. Exhaustion dragging him down. He was bruised, burned, and bloodied. He was alive. He had survived. He did it all for Autumn.

"We got him Autumn, we got him baby girl," Bryson whispered, as he stared into the night sky. Tears trickling down his cheeks from the outside corner of his eyes.

"We'll never be free of this, will we?" Bryson said softly, as he rolled over staring at the swamp. The question hung in the humid air, heavy as the moss draped over the cypress trees. The swamp, in its way, offered an answer, or rather, the illusion of one. A place of profound stillness, it wasn't just the absence of sound, but a living, breathing entity that swallowed sound and secrets alike. The rustle of leaves, the croak of a frog, even the thumping of his own heart felt muted, absorbed by the spongy air and the dense vegetation.

It was where things went to disappear. Not just physically, but metaphorically. The murky depths hid everything that the light couldn't touch, everything that society tried to ignore or bury. Rotting logs, fallen branches, discarded objects, and now, a body—all consumed by the swamp's insatiable appetite. For Bryson, though, this place had become something else entirely, something far more personal and painful. It had become a place of trauma, inextricably linked to loss and violence. Autumn had been found here, a victim of the swamp's cold, silent embrace, her life extinguished in the depths of its hidden waterways. And now, Silas, her killer, was destined to become part of the same muddy tapestry.

The water, dark and still, seemed to promise absolution, a cleansing that would wash away the blood and the guilt, just as it washed away the fallen leaves and debris. It offered the seductive illusion of erasing the consequences, of burying the truth beneath the surface where no one would ever find it. But Bryson knew better. Some things, once done, could never be washed away, no matter how deep the water or how thick the mud. Some stains seeped into the soul, leaving a permanent mark. Some screams echoed, forever haunting the spaces between the cypress knees.

He looked down at Silas's body, sprawled awkwardly on the damp earth. In death, Silas looked smaller, less intimidating, almost vulnerable. But Bryson knew that was just another illusion. This man, this killer, had stolen something precious, something irreplaceable. He had taken Autumn's life, and in doing so, he had torn a hole in Bryson's world that could never be fully mended. The weight of his actions settled heavily on Bryson's shoulders, a burden far heavier than Silas's physical form.

He knew what had to be done. The evidence, the body, everything had to vanish. He grabbed Silas by the ankles and began to drag him towards the edge of the swamp. The body was heavier than he expected, a dead weight that seemed to resist every inch of movement. His muscles strained, his breath coming in ragged gasps, each exhale fogging in the air. The muddy ground sucked at his bare feet, making each step a struggle, the squelching sound adding to the eerie symphony of the swamp.

Twigs snapped, branches scraped against his arms, and the air grew with the pungent smell of decay. He pulled, grunted, and strained, his body slick with sweat. The fight with Silas had taken its toll, leaving him bruised and battered, but he pushed through the pain. Finally, with a final, guttural grunt of exertion, he pulled Silas to the water's edge. The swamp received him without a ripple, just a soft plop as the body sank below the surface. For a little while, there was nothing but the still, dark water, reflecting the crescent moon in the sky. It looked peaceful, serene, as if it had swallowed the chaos and transformed it into something beautiful, something tranquil. But Bryson knew the truth. Beneath that deceptively calm surface, a world of decay and danger lurked.

He stood there for what felt like an eternity, chest heaving, trying to catch his breath. Then, a movement. A ripple in the water's placid surface. A pair of eyes, cold and ancient, broke the surface. A massive alligator, its scales like armored plates, rose silently from the depths. Its jaws opened wide, revealing rows of sharp, jagged teeth, a primal testament to the brutal realities of this place. It was a creature of the swamp, perfectly adapted to its harsh environment, a predator that knew no mercy and no remorse. In a flash, with a speed that belied its size, it swallowed Silas's body, the massive creature pulling him down into the murky depths. The water churned, a momentary whirlpool of violence, and then, a horrifying sound—a sickening crunch and tear. The water transmuted into a disturbing red, spreading like a gruesome bloom, then stilled again, as if nothing had happened. The alligator disappeared, taking Silas with it, returning to the depths. The surface became smooth again.

A brutal ending, but in a twisted way, it felt fitting. An eye for an eye. Silas had come to this place seeking to perpetuate harm and death, and now he had become a part of it, a part of the very ecosystem he sought to exploit. There was a strange, almost poetic justice in it, a symmetry that sent a shiver down Bryson's spine. Unable to watch any longer, unable to bear the visceral reality of what he had just witnessed. His stomach churned, and he fought the urge to vomit. He stumbled back, away from the water's edge, his legs feeling heavy and unsteady. He spotted Silas's truck parked nearby, its dark outline blending into the surroundings.

He climbed inside. The keys were still in the ignition, dangling there as if waiting for him. He started the engine, it broke the heavy silence of Big Cypress Swamp, shattering the stillness like glass. The headlights cut through the darkness, illuminating the twisted shapes of the trees. He glanced one last time at the water, at the dark, impenetrable surface that held its secrets close. He knew he was leaving more than just a body behind. He was leaving behind a part of himself, a part of his innocence, a part of his soul. He was leaving behind the secrets, the trauma, the guilt. But he knew in the back of his head, that he was going to carry all of that with him. The claw etched forever on his leg. The blood on his hands was invisible to the eye but he knew it was there. He drove away but the ghosts of the swamp were forever chiseled into his soul, the echoes of Silas's death forever ringing in his ears. And he knew, with certainty, that he would never truly be free of this place, not of its darkness and not of the memory that Autumn had said her last word there. It was in him now, and it would stay with him until the end of his days.

Chapter 35- Sage, Bryson & Antoine

Bryson sat on the edge of his bathtub, watching pink-tinged water circle the drain. He'd been scrubbing for twenty minutes, but he could still smell it—the swamp, the blood, the smoke from Silas's campfire. The brand on his leg throbbed with each heartbeat, the claw mark already blistering.

His hands wouldn't stop shaking.

He'd killed a man last night. Not in self-defense, not accidentally. He'd beaten Silas until his skull cracked, until blood pooled in the mud, until the life left his eyes. Then he'd watched an alligator tear the body apart.

And he'd felt nothing. Just... empty.

The sun was rising now, orange light creeping through the bathroom window. He should call someone.

Antoine. Sage. His mother. But what would he say? Hey, I murdered someone last night and fed him to a gator. What's for breakfast?

His phone buzzed on the sink. Twenty-three missed calls. Fifteen texts. Most from Antoine. The last one, from ten minutes ago: WHERE THE FUCK ARE YOU

Bryson typed back with water-wrinkled fingers: *Home. I'm okay.*

The response was immediate: STAY THERE. ON MY WAY.

Nahh, I'll come by yo crib. Bryson responded

Bryson set the phone down, looked at himself in the mirror. The man staring back was a stranger. Bruised jaw. Bloodshot eyes. A hardness in his expression that hadn't been there yesterday. He'd gone into that swamp one person and come out another.

The question was: which one was real?

Bryson arrived at the trailer an hour later. Antoine stood in the doorway, arms crossed, expression unreadable. "Is he dead?"

Bryson nodded.

"You sure?"

"The gator was sure," said Bryson.

Silence. Sage sat down beside Bryson, her hand finding his. Antoine moved to the window, looked out at the brightening morning, then closed the blinds.

Knowing the truth didn't fill the void. It didn't bring Autumn back.

They sat in silence for a long moment. Outside, birds were singing. A car drove past. Normal sounds, normal morning. But nothing was normal anymore. "The truck," Bryson said suddenly. "Silas's truck. I drove it away from the swamp, left it near the docks. We need to get rid of it."

"Let's go burn that shit! No prints, no evidence, no connection to you," emphasized Antoine.

Bryson stared at the floor. Then he glanced at the branding of the claw on his leg.

"So," Bryson said finally. "What now?"

Antoine shrugged and took a swig of his beer. "Hell, now we live with it. We got the answers, we took care of business, now it's time to move on, my boy. We told the police what we knew. It's their job now," Antoine smirked. "We can't fix everything. It's the swamp's secret now."

Epilogue: Three Months Later

Bryson sat across from Detective Mason in the interview room. The fluorescent lights hummed overhead, the same mechanical drone that had filled his prison cell years ago.

Mason slid a photo across the table—a grainy still from a traffic camera. A Ram 1500, timestamp: 3:47 AM, the night Silas disappeared.

"We tracked this truck from the swamp to the docks. Watched it burn on security footage." Mason tapped the photo. "But here's the thing—we found Silas's phone records. Last ping was near your house. Two hours before this truck showed up at the fire."

Bryson kept his breathing steady. "You already know he kidnapped me. I told you everything."

"You told us a story," Mason corrected. "Man breaks into your house, brands you, drags you to the swamp, then conveniently gets eaten by a gator while you escape. That's a hell of a story."

"It's the truth."

Mason pulled out another photo. This one showed Bryson's neighborhood. A streetlight. A timestamp. "Your neighbor's Ring camera. Shows Silas's truck leaving your house at 2:14 AM. You know what it doesn't show?"

Bryson waited.

"It doesn't show anyone following it. Doesn't show how you got from the swamp back to civilization. Doesn't show how a man who was nearly dead from torture managed to burn a truck so thoroughly that forensics found nothing." Mason leaned forward. "Help me understand that."

The silence stretched between them like swamp water—dark, thick, hiding what lay beneath.

"I walked," Bryson said finally. "From the swamp. Found a road. Called a ride."

"At 4 AM? After being beaten and branded? With no phone records to support it?"
"Sometimes the truth sounds impossible."

Mason studied him for a long moment. Then he closed the folder and stood.

"You know what keeps me up at night, Bryson? It's not that I can't prove what I know. It's that part of me doesn't want to." He paused at the door. "Sterling was a drug dealer. Bugsy and Junior were killers. Silas... he was a ghost who left bodies in the swamp. And now they're gone. Case closed. Everyone's happy."

"Except you."

"Except me," Mason agreed. "Because I became a cop to enforce the law. Not to decide who deserves to die." He looked back at Bryson. "The difference between justice and revenge? Justice doesn't keep you up at night."

After Mason left, Bryson sat alone in the too-bright room. He pulled up his pant leg, looked at the claw brand scarred into his skin. The flesh had healed, but the mark remained—permanent, raised, a map of that night written on his body.

He thought about Autumn. About Gabriel growing up without a mother. About his own hands, the things they'd done.

Tag, you're it.

The words weren't Silas's anymore. They belonged to him now—a game that never ended, passed from victim to killer to victim again. An inheritance of violence that the swamp had witnessed for centuries, long before him.

He pressed his thumb against the brand, felt the ridge of scar tissue.

Outside, Sage was waiting in her car. Antoine had texted: *Cleared?*

Bryson texted back: *For now.*

But as he walked toward the exit, past the bulletin board with its missing persons flyers and cold case photos, he wondered if anyone was ever really cleared. Not from guilt. Not from the swamp's memory. Not from the secrets it kept.

He pushed through the door into the Florida heat, into the bright lie of a normal day. Behind him, the police station hummed with bureaucratic life—reports filed, cases closed, justice served.

The swamp knew better.

It always did.

Author's Notes

The Calusa: The People Behind the Setting

When you step into the Everglades through the pages of this novel, you are also walking into the homeland of the Calusa. Their name has often been translated as *fierce people*, and for centuries they ruled the southwest coast of Florida with strength, skill, and spirit.

A Life Shaped by Water

The Calusa did not plant vast fields of crops the way many other Native peoples did. Instead, they lived by the tides, currents, and rivers. The sea and wetlands were their farms. They cast wide nets for fish, gathered oysters and clams, and hunted sea turtles and manatees.

Over generations, they built great shell mounds and canals, reshaping the landscape itself. Some of these mounds became platforms for homes and temples, rising above the watery world around them. Even today, traces of their engineering still mark the land.

Beliefs and Traditions

The Calusa saw the world through a spiritual lens. They believed every person had three souls—one in the pupil, one in the shadow, and one in the reflection. Leaders held not only political power but also spiritual authority, guiding ceremonies that honored both nature and the unseen.

Their rituals and traditions gave order and meaning to life in the Everglades, connecting the people to the waters that sustained them.

Encounters with Strangers

The first Europeans to set foot in Florida—led by Juan Ponce de León in 1513—met the Calusa. But they did not meet them as friends. The Calusa resisted colonization fiercely, turning back ships and missionaries alike.

Despite their strength, new diseases, slave raids, and centuries of conflict eventually took their toll. By the 1700s, the Calusa were gone as a distinct people, their survivors scattered across Florida or carried away to Cuba.

Their Enduring Legacy

Though their voices are quiet now, the Calusa left a mark that endures in Florida's history. Their shell mounds, canals, and artifacts still whisper of a people who mastered the waters of the Everglades and Gulf Coast.

To learn about the Calusa is to see the Everglades differently—not only as a wild landscape, but as a home, a kingdom, and a spiritual world for those who came before.

For Curious Readers

- Florida Museum of Natural History – Calusa Exhibit

- The Calusa and Their Legacy: South Florida People and Their Environments by Darcie A. MacMahon and William H. Marquardt

SECRETS THE SWAMP KEEPS

ACKNOWLEDGEMENTS

Late nights, early mornings. Wine, candles, jazz music, prayers.

What was just an idea became a three-dimensional object. Won't he do it!?

I give all the glory and honor to the man above, without him none of this would've been possible. Thank you, Lord, for always directing me in your will.

I am eternally grateful.

Also, I thank myself for never giving up.

ABOUT THE AUTHOR

Jon-Patric Nelson is a Jamaican-born writer with a doctorate in physical therapy. When he's not crafting suspenseful, atmospheric fiction, he can be found enjoying the laid-back company of his loyal dog, Onyx. Jon-Patric's stories often explore the resilience of ordinary people facing extraordinary darkness—and the secrets that places, families, and communities keep buried.

Email: jonpatricnelson@gmail.com
Instagram: @jonpatricnelson